Mary Finch Endgame

S S Saywack was born in Guyana in 1955 and now lives in London, United Kingdom. He has published a number of books including the Mary Finch Mysteries, of which this book is the first, and has won a number of awards.

ALSO BY S S SAYWACK

Mary Finch and the Thief

Mary Finch and the Grey Lady

Mary Finch and the Spy

Mary Finch Endgame

Mary Finch Runaway, a prologue

Perdita, the Witch and the Toyshop

Inglestone Manor

Available as both eBooks and print books.

S S SAYWACK

Mary Finch Endgame

A Mary Finch Mystery

First published 2022

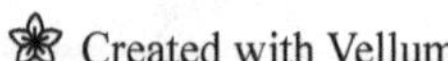 Created with Vellum

For my sisters, brother and mum,
for all their support over the years.

Fog everywhere. Fog up the river where it flows among green airs and meadows; fog down the river, where it rolls defiled among the tiers of shipping, and the waterside pollutions of a great (and dirty) city.

Charles Dickens, Bleak House

I

❧ I ❧

A LONDON PARTICULAR

PERHAPS IT WAS THE FOG, and the menacing quality fog brings, that made the hairs on the back of Mary Finch's neck prickle. But she could swear she heard footsteps behind her that stopped abruptly when she did. Then, when she glanced back, she saw a ghostly figure, a shape only, slide silently into the mist.

A London Particular, a yellow-brown, sulphurous fog, was busy snuffing out the light, threatening to make the night as black as pitch. The clock had not long struck six in the evening. It was as bleak a December day as she had ever known, and it was Arctic cold.

Mary leant her head forward and screwed up her eyes, and peered into the gloom. Nothing could be seen. The fetid mustard-grey wall, like a curtain, lazily folded over itself in the light breeze. She walked on a few more yards only to stop again to listen.

The footsteps were gone. There were no other sounds but the of snorting horses and the wheels of carriages dully grinding across the roadway, and the drivers' muffled warnings to whoever was ahead of them.

Stop being stupid, she said to herself, *it's just what's happened recently and to poor Archie that's making you second guess everything.* It was probably someone going home, and travelling in the same direction, Mary convinced herself. She rubbed her side where a cut ached dully, remembering how she got it, and hurried on. It was too cold to hang about.

A few paces only and there they were again: the steady rhythm of footsteps keeping pace with her. The realisation that she was being followed made her skin crawl. A cold shiver trembled her. Mary glanced over her shoulder nervously.

Nothing but the mustard-grey curtain.

She crossed the street, fearful of the carriages she could not see in the fog.

Holding her breath, Mary listened closely. But it felt as if her ears were stuffed with cotton wool. She could not hear the footsteps. Mary exhaled in relief. It was easy to mistake sounds in the fog, especially as this business she was involved in was making her nervous. She chided herself, she was imagining things only, no more than that.

Mary walked on, but quicker now.

As she did, the news of the murder of Charles

Augustus Milverton, the master blackmailer, came back to her. Mary shivered as she did then when she first glimpsed the headlines. It was the day she walked through the door of Deacon House. A strange sense of foreboding come to her then. It felt as if she'd been visited by a ghost. The memory added to her nervousness and she hurried on, feeling the same dread as when she first read the news.

Despite the blindfold of fog, Mary knew where she was going. The route to the lodging house she recently moved into was firmly imprinted on her mind. It lay a little way ahead, just across Westminster Bridge in Lambeth.

From around her, she heard once more the slow clip-clopping of hooves, the heavy breathing of horses, wheels grinding on the cobbles and the drivers' muffled voices all lost in the gloom. Dull pools of yellow light drifted past her from the lanterns carried by the carriages; ghostly shadows and shapes dawdled past. Slowly her mind returned to what happened in Oxford Street and to poor Archie, the strange look on Inspector Baynes's face. They closed out other thoughts.

Then there they were again, the steady beat of foot-fall, metal capped boots clicking on the cobblestones, several yards behind her. Mary glance behind her and a shape slipped back into the fog. Her heart raced and her breathing quickened. Panicking, Mary sped up. Had she been followed since meeting her friends in Trafalgar

Square? The clicking steps said yes. Stumbling, unsure of what lay ahead, she hurried to get away.

The footsteps followed.

Now she was running, blindly running. She went as fast as she could, mindful that she could see nothing ahead of her. Her heart was thumping, her breathing came in quick, sharp gasps. She was halfway across Westminster Bridge when Mary suddenly stopped and turned swiftly. The footsteps stopped just as abruptly. Big Ben rang out the quarter, the chimes muffled in the fuggy air.

'Who's there?' she shouted.

Her eyes jerked sideways.

She strained her ears.

Not a sound other than the slow grinding of carriage wheels, the wheezing of horses, their snorting breaths, the gurgling of the Thames beneath her.

'Come on, show yourself. I know someone's there.'

She listened intently.

Nothing.

Fearful of the dreadful silence, she began to back away whilst holding her breath. Despite the cold, she was hot, her face and neck damp with perspiration. Now all she could hear was her pounding heart, blood swooshing in her ears, her chattering teeth. Then her heart froze. From inside the dense, foul-smelling mustard curtain, from behind her, the slow clip-clopping of metal on stone was coming closer. Mary spun around just as a figure loomed out of the fog and clattered into her. She screamed. Two hands grasped her elbows, and, as she fell backwards, they pulled her upright.

She was looking into the startled eyes of a small, elderly gentleman.

'S-sorry, miss. A-are you all right? I-I didn't mean to scare you,' he stammered.

'Blimey, mister.' Mary, her racing heart almost exploding, gasped in relief. 'You did that all right!' She swallowed her fears. A watery smile trembled her lips, and an anxious, nervous laugh slipped out.

'S-sorry,' he said again and released her elbows. 'I couldn't see a thing—'

'Me neither,' Mary said. 'Blimey! That's got me ticker going,' she joked.

'Are you sure you are alright?' he asked kindly.

When Mary nodded. He tipped his hat and generously stepped to one side allowing her to pass. Mary slipped away. Her heart, though, continued to thump loudly. She went a few steps, stopped to wipe the perspiration off her face with a handkerchief, and dab around the hair at the back of her neck which was now chilly with sweat. She heard the old man's footsteps fade and vanish deep inside the fog.

'Get a grip of yourself, Finch,' she whispered, wishing to hear a voice, even if it were only her own. Heaving a sigh of relief and drawing her coat tighter, Mary started off again.

The sudden staccato clacking of footsteps was like a drum roll reaching a crescendo. Mary just had time to swing around and see a dark figure loom out of the mist. Before she could speak, two strong arms lifted her up and off the ground. She was being carried to the side of the bridge, towards the river. Mary kicked her legs and swung her fists in desperation.

'Help! Help!' she shouted, just as her back slammed into the railing. She was being lifted up and over them. In desperation Mary gripped the cold, greasy rail tightly, hanging on for dear life. A hand grasped hers, nails digging into her flesh, pinching at her grip. She heard a grunted curse as her hands were pulled away.

'Help! Help!'

It was hopeless. No matter how much she twisted and squirmed to get free, she was being tilted, further and further over the edge. Below her, the swirling icy water of the Thames slap-slapped gurgling against the piles, waited for her, opening its arms to welcome her.

'Help! *Help!*' Mary screamed.

2

MANY PARTINGS

SEVERAL WEEKS EARLIER.

'NOW, YOU ARE SURE THIS IS WHAT YOU WANT?' MRS Grady asked.

The old woman, who was well past sixty and, up until a week ago, Mary's employer, dismounted her carriage. She brushed her red hair away from her eyes to glare at the building in front of her. Perhaps she couldn't believe what she was seeing. The soot-blackened bricks with peeling paint and the rotten window frames told their own tale. And a sorrowful one indeed, judging by the look on her face. The building was old and shabby, a far cry from Mrs Grady's splendid house, the Rose Garden, in Holland Park. This four-storey structure certainly saw better days.

'It's perfect,' Mary said. She wore a pasted-on smile. Deep down, however, she was regretful, leaving her lovely warm room that gazed across the pleasant green space of Holland Park for an attic room with a kitchen and views across the smoking chimney tops of Lambeth. But she couldn't tell the old lady that.

As lodgings go, it was the best she could afford without dipping into her savings. Nevertheless, she felt a certain pride. Mary was about to become an independent woman, though perhaps at fourteen, she was hardly a woman as such. While the accommodation gave the appearance of a demotion in fortune, Mary comforted herself knowing that at last she was no longer a maid, and this was the price for that privilege.

The old lady pursed her lips contemptuously, and muttered under her breath, *Lambeth of all places!'* She huffed quietly and turned her gaze southwards, and Mary knew where she was looking: Bethlem Royal Hospital for the insane lay not a half mile away. At that moment, Mary knew exactly what the old lady was thinking.

'Well, Lambeth's good enough for the Archbishop, Mrs Grady,' Mary said brightly, and nodded in the direction of Lambeth Palace, the Archbishop's residence, also a half mile away. Mrs Grady snorted under her breath, clearly not impressed by the Archbishop's choice of location.

'I am sorry to lose you,' Mrs Grady said, 'but I would have wished...' she trailed off into silence. She resigned herself to the facts, shook her head slowly and turned to face Mary. 'No. This is how it must be, Mary, if you are *sure* this is what you want.'

Mary gave her a beaming smile.

'I am, Mrs Grady. Really.'

'Yes.' Mrs Grady nodded. 'Yes. I can see that.'

There was a certain unmistakable pride in the old lady's eyes of her former maid that Mary couldn't help but notice. Despite appearances, Mary had improved herself, as they both knew she would.

'Things have changed, ma'am,' Mary said.

'They have indeed. Now, this man, this Major… Major…?'

'Carshaw.'

'Yes, this Major Carshaw. He is paying you suffi-cient? Your salary is adequate?'

'It is, ma'am. Quite adequate. Honestly.' She would have to scrimp. But he promised to increase her salary if she could prove herself as a— what was it he called it? A suitable candidate? A challenge was the spur she needed.

'I see. But the job is not a position in his household? Which is why you must find accommodation nearby.'

'Yes, ma'am. It's in his… well, I think you'd call it his business.'

'And that business is?'

'Something to do with the… the government,' Mary said evasively.

'Something to do with the government,' Mrs Grady

repeated blankly. 'And he was the man you met in the summer?'

'With Mr Holmes's brother, Mycroft, ma'am.'

'The ones who had something to do with *your* brother?'

Mary nodded.

'Finding Daniel a job abroad, you said.'

'Yes, Mrs Grady.' Though what that *job* was, she could not tell her.

'And this position he has offered you… you do not yet know what it entails… your duties, I mean?'

'Not fully, ma'am. I'm to be told properly on Monday.'

'Tomorrow. I see.' The old lady turned her back to Mary and gazed across the street. She fiddled with her sleeve and withdrew a lace handkerchief and grasped it tightly in her hand.

'Well, do not just sit there, young man,' Mrs Grady said sharply to Archie Dibble, Mary's friend, who was seated in the carriage along with another young girl. 'Get Mary's luggage to her rooms. Come on.' Archie, a hefty boy of sixteen, quickly dismounted, and quietly smiled at the old lady's pretend anger. The driver followed him to the back of the carriage. 'And Mary, make sure you unpack quickly, otherwise your clothes will have creases. The sheets will need an airing. You have an iron… and pots… and…? There is a wardrobe, I suppose?'

'Iron and pots, ma'am. Cook and Mr Venables made sure. And there is furniture.'

'Good. I should hope so.'

She was grateful that Mrs Grady's cook, Eileen, and the butler, Mr Venables, purchased items for her. *There are things that a young, independent lady will need,* they said.

Mary stood awkwardly beside the old woman, not sure if she should hug her, which is what she wanted to do for all her kindness, or just shake her hand, though that seemed impersonal and cold. Of the three people whom she worked for, Mrs Grady was by far the best. She was treated less as a maid and more as a member of her family. She suspected there were few households in the whole of London, not to mention England, where such informality reigned, as it did in Mrs Grady's house.

The old lady turned her gaze to the inside of the carriage, where the young girl was energetically scratching her legs.

'Kitty, will you stop doing that—it is most unlady-like,' Mrs Grady said.

'It itches me pins,' Kitty moaned.

'It itches *my legs*,' Mrs Grady corrected her.

'That's what I said,' Kitty replied. 'Why can't I wear me breeches? This itches like I've got fleas or something.'

'Young ladies do not wear breeches under any circumstances. As for fleas …' Mrs Grady sighed loudly.

'It would not surprise me. Now help Archie take some items to Mary's rooms.'

The ten-year-old girl Mary met in the summer, had her nose, eyes, and mouth tightly screwed up and was scratching her legs through the cotton stockings she wore. Until recently, she was a member of Sherlock Holmes's Baker Street Irregulars, street urchins the great detective sometimes employed to aid his investigations. Kitty Short-Pants, as she was known for her habit of wearing breeches, had respectability—she now worked as one of Mrs Grady's maids.

Kitty climbed down from the carriage. Instead of her customary breeches, she wore a smart, long-sleeved navy-blue dress, white cotton stockings, and shiny, black, flat-heeled shoes. Her hair was tied in a pony-tail gathered neatly with a bow made of red satin. She was a far cry from the dirty-faced urchin Mary remembered.

She ran to the back of the carriage and stood beside a hefty case. Before picking it up, she sniffed, swiped her sleeve across her nose, then spat into her palms and vigorously rubbed them together. Mrs Grady stiffened, and Mary almost burst out laughing as the old lady gazed heavenwards, then closed her eyes as if offering up a silent prayer.

'Thanks for looking after Kitty, Mrs Grady,' Mary said before the old lady could speak.

Mrs Grady nodded slightly.

'Now that Fortune has taken over your position, I

need someone to take over hers.' Mrs Grady sighed loudly once more as she watched Kitty walk past, struggling with the case, but gamely persevering. 'I can see that one will be challenging.'

'I'm gonna miss you, Mrs Grady,' Mary said. 'And Cook's dinners. And Mr Venables polishing the silver when I should be doing it. Ella as well. And I'm gonna miss Fortune and Oscar.'

'*That cat* has already moved on—and straight into Fortune's room, I noticed.'

'And I can't thank you enough—'

'Hush, child! The Rose Garden will always be open to you. I expect you to come and take tea with us. And I *shall* see you at Christmas.' Once more Mrs Grady surveyed the tall, grim, soot-covered building. 'You will not spend Christmas here, but with us,' she said softly as if to herself.

'I'd like that very much, ma'am.'

'The Dibbles shall come as well. Yes, they shall. Sally and Dorothy and Archie and their grandparents. We shall have a special celebration.' Mary thought she saw a shadow pass across the old lady's face, a regret perhaps at their parting, but she could not be certain. 'And we shall invite Ella's mother and grandmother. Yes, they should be there as well. Ella might be my ward, but they are her family, and Christmas is a time for families. And I believe that Kitty has a brother—he too shall come.'

'Are you all right, ma'am?' Mary asked and took the

old lady's hands. She seemed frail. A ghost of herself only, that in the excitement of leaving to take up her new employment, Mary had failed to noticed.

'Why do you ask? Do I not look all right?' Mrs Grady said loudly. She stood upright, shaking off the shadow.

'It's just that I wanted to say—'

'Hush,' Mrs Grady said, opening her arms wide. Drawing Mary closer, she hugged her tightly.

The old lady felt thin, nothing more than skin and bones, and Mary detected a slight tremble.

'Do you remember me once saying that my best years lay behind me while yours lay ahead, and how we could help each other?' Mrs Grady asked.

'Like it was yesterday.'

'I liked you from that very first day when you came to my house with Ella and the Dibble children. I think I saw me in you. Yes, that is what I think I saw.'

Mary blushed, stuttered, and said nothing. The old lady was smiling at her.

'Did I ever mention where I was born?' she asked.

'In Ireland, wasn't it?'

'In County Kerry. That is in the south. In the Dingle peninsular. We had a house on the coast.' Mrs Grady stopped speaking and released Mary. She edged back inside her carriage. Sitting down, she drew her coat tighter around her shoulders as if the cold December air was finally affecting her. She eased back against the rest. 'Of late, I have often wondered what happened to the house that overlooked the sea. I have sometimes wondered who lives in it, if indeed it was still there. In my dreams, I smell the air, fresh with salt. And when the storms blow in from the Atlantic—'

A shadow passed across the old lady's face, and Mary, feeling concerned, thought she should say something. Before she could, Mrs Grady smiled and in the sparkle of the smile, the shadow vanished.

'It is best you go and see they have not broken anything,' she said softly. 'Men are such clumsy creatures. As for Kitty… And I shall expect you for tea. If not tea, then for Christmas.'

With that, the old lady eased the carriage door shut and sat gazing out of the window to the opposite side of the street. An air of melancholy surrounded her. She screwed her lace handkerchief up tightly in her hand, working her fist around it, and was silent.

3

AN ACCOUNTING

WHEN EVERYONE LEFT, Mary was finally alone with her thoughts. She exhaled a long breath. Lying to Mrs Grady, the woman who'd been so kind to her, made her feel awful. It wasn't a lie, Mary told herself, not a real lie. She'd just not told her everything. She knew only too well it was a lie by omission—she wasn't stupid.

Things moved quickly since receiving Major Carshaw's letter. The major, who worked for the British Secret Service, an organisation she didn't know existed until recently, was impressed with her when they first met, during the summer. But, Mary surmised, it was probably the person they were with, Mycroft Holmes, the elder brother of the great detective, Sherlock, who was really impressed. *'Maybe you should employ Miss Finch, Major. You could do worse,'* he said, almost jokingly, when Mary figured out a plan the major thought secret. It was, no doubt, on his suggestion that she was offered a 'situation'.

You are invited to report for employment at the above address at nine a.m. on the 4th December 1893.
Yours sincerely,
Major J T Carshaw DSO, IGSM (India)

How could she refuse?

Now that she found her brother, and lost him at the same time, she felt a change had come. A fresh wind was blowing in her sails and she felt its irresistible force pushing her away from her old life and into something new. She was running with the tide, and to stay would be to deny herself. Her fingertips tingled and her feet fidgeted with the anticipation it brought. She had to succumb. She knew that the old lady would be the first to advise her to follow where it led. Even so, she felt awful that she'd lied to her.

'What we do is a secret, Miss Finch,' the major impressed on her. 'No one must know—for their sake as well as ours. Remember your brother.'

She did. Daniel Finch was in Germany. She didn't know what exactly he was doing, only that he was employed by the major and that meant it was a dangerous game he was playing. She knew only too well the meaning of the word espionage, enough to know that it was now Daniel's game. And now she, too, was asked to join the sport.

She'd fretted before she felt brave enough to inform Mrs Grady of her intentions, thinking in some ways she was letting her down. Of course, that was nonsense, as she knew only too well. If anything, Mrs Grady would positively encourage her if it meant she was improving herself. When they first met, Mary told the old lady she planned to better herself. Mrs Grady replied, *'Good, because I would have it no other way.'*

Mary assumed many years would pass before those plans could be realised, not a few months instead. Her time in Mrs Grady's employment unfurled itself in unusual ways. What distressed her was that she could not tell anyone anything about the position being offered to her. The terms of employment, the major insisted, forbade any disclosure. It placed her in the most unusual and inconvenient of predicaments.

This, though, was her chance to be independent, to live her own life and not beholden to anyone, a chance to progress from being a maid to... well, that she wasn't sure—nor exactly what her *situation* was. In fact, there was much she didn't know. Only, here she was, the *great Lady Mary Finch* of her daydreams, a private, self-supporting citizen. The pride she felt was mixed with the sadness of leaving her friends behind.

Now, sitting on her bed, she surveyed her new kingdom. It wasn't much. A far cry from the luxury of the

Rose Garden. It was no more than a bedsitting room with another that passed as a kitchen. The bed was a single cot, pushed up against a wall. A small table next to it acted as a night stand. Another table with two chairs was beside the window, its glass grimy. Mary reminded herself that she would give it a wash before the week was out. There was a thin square of carpet on the floor, and the boards creaked with each step. A small tatty couch stood on it. Against another wall was a wardrobe and a dresser, and beside that was an empty bookcase.

Off the room was the small compact kitchen. It had a sink, a spirit stove, some cupboards, and a small table to work on. The only other window in the flat was also grimy.

The bathroom was on the dark landing below, and shared with the occupants of that floor. The unmistakable odours of stale cabbage, fried food, and sour milk wafted up the stairwell.

No pets were allowed, not that she could keep one. It would be most cruel in this place, because there was no access to an outside space, a garden on some such. She would miss Oscar, her cat, dearly.

In all honesty, this accommodation wasn't the one she would have wished for herself. But needs must she knew to be true. After all, she lived in worst places, so, she could stand living here for a while. When she was very young, she and her foster family moved briefly to Liverpool, where they lived in absolute squalor. Even though she could afford someplace better, she was determined to hold on to the money she'd saved, and that given to her by her brother. Mary had plans for the future, and she would need the cash then. With any increase of salary, she promised herself, she would find someplace much better to live. Until then, she would manage on what she earned.

She arose and began to put away her possessions. Things went into drawers, were hung on hooks, and in the wardrobe. She stowed her treasures on the small dresser—these were photographs of her parents, images of people she barely remembered who died when she was three-years-old, a bundle of letters written by her mother and father to each other, along with a few other items. And lastly, she placed her mother's heart-shaped locket, now repaired, having once been divided in two, on the dresser as well. One half had been given to her, the other to her brother.

As she worked, she reflected how quickly things change.

Towards the end of last winter, she was employed by Mr Grimwig of Regent's Park, until she was wrongfully accused of theft. Her success, in proving her innocence by catching the thief, had been his downfall and exposed him for what he was—a blackmailer, amongst other things. His butler, Mr Boots, even tried to kill her.

Afterwards, she found employment with Mrs Grady.

A kinder person she didn't know, unless it was her friends, the Dibbles.

Then, in the summer, she met Mr Boots again. By chance he was 'working' with her brother. Daniel Finch was painted as an anarchist, murderer, and a desperate criminal. Later, she discovered the clever ruse hatched by Mycroft Holmes and Major Carshaw, and the role of spy that they'd assigned to Daniel. Mr Boots was now languishing in jail. And now, because of her cleverness, she too was being courted by the major. But for what, she didn't know. The game was keeping secrets; the trick was knowing them and not telling them.

She exhaled loudly thinking about how she'd lied to Mrs Grady, and for the lies she would have to tell her best friend, Archie Dibble.

As she climbed into bed that night, much had changed in so short a time. She was being carried along by uncertain currents into an uncertain future. But she would have it no other way. Uncertain as the future was, it was a country she longed to explore.

Mary yawned, drew the blankets around her tightly against the pinching cold and gazed into the darkness of her room. She was restless with anticipation. What was it Mr Holmes said to his friend that day? Oh, yes, that was it: *Education never ends, Watson. It is a series of lessons, with the greatest for the last.'*

4

A HOUSE NEAR WHITEHALL

THE NEXT DAY, on Monday morning, Mary walked from her rooms and across Westminster Bridge. There was a bounce in her steps. She checked the time on a small pocket watch, a present from Mr Venables, against the time on the clockface of Westminster tower in front of her. She derived a deep shudder of satisfaction from seeing that the time on her watch was the same as that on the tower. She wore the watch with pride; the chain threaded through a buttonhole on her lapel and secured with a fob, the mechanism resting in a small breast pocket. Mr Venables paid her the compliment of saying the trinket would set her apart and mark her as a young woman of distinction. She'd blushed scarlet. Yet as she walked, head held high, passing people going to their places of employment, Mary felt it keenly—just what it must be like to be considered a young woman of distinction.

She passed Westminster Bridge underground station and the Houses of Parliament before turning into Parliament Street. That led her into the wide avenue of Whitehall, with Downing Street nearby, where the prime minister resided. Elegant cream-coloured buildings flanked the avenue, dark windows overlooked her, and a feeling of pride fluttered through her heart with thoughts that *this* was where she was to be employed—somewhere in one of these magnificent edifices from where Britain and her Empire were governed.

It was unexpected then to be confronted by a quiet and sober, soot-blackened building in a side street off Whitehall, not unlike the one where she now lived, squeezed between other sober, soot-blackened buildings. If Whitehall shouted pomp and ceremony, this whispered anonymity. An undistinguished brass plaque, etched with the words *Deacon House*, gleamed next to the door.

A uniformed doorman, a swarthy man with a face that had seen trouble in all its forms, was seated behind the entrance. He was a large man and the desk, a large piece of furniture, appeared pathetically small in front of him. Even seated, his eyes were level with Mary's. He was reading a newspaper, and Mary noticed the headlines on the front page reporting the death of Charles Augustus Milverton.

A feeling of unease came over her when she read the

name. After all this time, she was surprised that the memory was still fresh. She shuddered.

Mary met him only twice. The first time she'd mistaken him for a lawyer, sent by Mr Grimwig to threaten her. She remembered his quiet grey eyes and the menace they held. But the second time, she knew him for what he was. Inspector Lestrade of Scotland Yard informed her his profession in the mistaken belief that she was in Milverton's employment, working together to blackmail her old employer, Mr Grimwig.

It was only through her quick thinking that she and Archie got away by the skin of their teeth from the man Grimwig sent to retrieve his possession, an assassin named Black Bob; and only then by playing a dangerous game and claiming she was, after all, working with Milverton. She nearly died that day when she had to jump into the Thames to escape him. All her old fears about drowning were resurgent, and for many months afterwards her dreams were suffused with the horror she felt at that time.

But it was Milverton's serpentine smile that she remembered when she refused his suggestion that she should work for him in blackmailing her then new employer, Mrs Grady.

'And conscience is such a luxury, especially for one with a limited income,' he said at the time.

At least mine's clear, Mary said, *limited income or none at all.*

So, the master blackmailer was dead. No one would miss him, except his victims. And they would do so cheerfully, and, no doubt, celebrate his passing.

Mary was so lost in her thoughts, she didn't notice the doorman place his newspaper down to gaze at her suspiciously. His stare was unblinking.

'Yes?' he asked curtly.

Taken unawares by both his directness and the news report, Mary fumbled inside her bag and withdrew a letter sent to her by the major. He scrutinised her carefully, took the letter in one gigantic paw, the knuckles calloused and scarred, and read it distrustfully. He even held it up to the light. Satisfied, he charged a young lad, not quite Mary's age, to escort her up a staircase to a room deep inside the building.

The boy, with a puppy-fat face and spikey blond hair, made a show of carrying her letter, waving it to say *this way*. Mary followed him nervously.

She'd kept her fears in check until that moment. Now, walking down unfamiliar corridors, passing portraits of people she didn't know but knew were important, who gazed at her contemptuously, they surfaced. She felt hot and uncomfortable and was suddenly eager to be elsewhere. Why she thought she could do this, she didn't know anymore. She was a maid, and a good one. She had a fine position in a wonderful household, a situation many would envy. All she had to do was stop the boy, say she'd changed her mind, turn and go, secure in the knowledge that Mrs Grady would give her back her old position at the drop of a hat.

Mary shook her head. No, she had to do this. Chances like this didn't come often.

'I'm Mary, by the way,' she said brightly to the boy, trying to lift her spirits. The boy carried an air of quiet contempt and walked swiftly on without replying. 'Well, pardon me for speaking,' Mary whispered under her breath.

The maze of corridors they walked were a dark and shadowy warren, weakly lit by single gas lamps at various points. The carpet was deep, her footsteps soundless. She passed various doors, each with a brass plaque detailing the names and positions of so-and-so and such-and-such, all done in silence.

It seemed an age before the boy stopped at a door at the end of a long corridor and knocked. There was no plaque on this door. A second later, a familiar voice said, 'Enter,' and the boy opened the door and went in. Mary followed.

Major Carshaw stood by the window.

Several months ago, not long after her brother, Danny Finch, had departed the country, the major interviewed her. He'd made vague references to a situation he said would be of interest to her. He was circumspect and told her little other than it was important. Then he sent her a letter of introduction and an offer of a position. It was an offer she felt she couldn't refuse. Now, standing there, she wondered again at her wisdom—giving up sure employment for something vague.

The major, a tall, lean man with a military bearing and sporting a thin moustache, was holding a tightly rolled up umbrella by the metal tip, the curved wooden handle resting on the floor beside a small white ball. On the other side of the room, on the floor, were similar white balls and a mug resting on its side, the opening facing the major.

'Miss Finch, sir,' the boy said brightly. He placed Mary's letter of introduction on the desk with a flourish.

'Thank you, Tiggs. Close the door on your way out; now there's a good boy,' the major said, somewhat rudely and unperturbed.

As the boy left, the major carefully swung the handle of his umbrella and struck the ball that trundled across the carpet towards the cup. Before reaching it, the ball swerved to the right, missing the cup by a good twelve inches. The major grumbled his disappointment. His finger came up and he smoothed his thin moustache. He looked at Mary and with a flick of his head, indicated for her to go to the desk where a document lay.

'Read,' he said simply, and went and retrieved the balls lying beside the cup.

Mary picked up the document. It was headed: *An Act To Prevent The Disclosure Of Official Documents And Information; 1889.* It was several pages long. It took some minutes to digest, by which time the major struck and retrieved his golf balls on two occasions. When she finished, she turned back to the major.

'Now, sign,' he said condescendingly.

She did.

'Everything about this building,' the major said while looking down and concentrating on the golf ball he was about to strike, 'about what you see and hear whilst you are here, about what you think whilst in our employ, about who you meet, where you meet, when you meet, why you meet, even how you meet, is now subject to law. Should you disclose any such information to a third party without our consent, we shall prosecute. We will lock you away in the Tower of London and throw away the key. And there you will rot and become food for the rats. Is it understood?'

Mary swallowed nervously and nodded.

'It had better be, Miss Finch,' The major said, looking up.

'Yes, sir.' Mary took a deep breath, briefly closed her eyes and tried to relax. She wondered just what she'd gotten herself into.

The major retrieved the letter of introduction he sent her, and casually deposited it into the flames in the fireplace. He paused to watch it burn. Suddenly, the room felt stuffy and overly warm, and Mary became hot and edgy, desperately wanting to remove her coat.

'The document you have signed gives us that power. Yes, Miss Finch. It is the same one your brother signed.

Now, make no mistake. This business is serious, and you are no fool to not know that. What you are about to embark on is a secret. No one knows of us, not least of all *the bald-headed man on the London Omnibus.* That way, we work better. It is safer, as well. If it is your wish, you are free to leave us now; we will not see you again, and you will not see us again. We have your signature that you will not disclose this meeting, and that will be the end of it. But if you stay—' he tapped the document sharply with a finger—'then be aware of the stipulations. We take them seriously. And we bite, Miss Finch.'

Once more, Mary swallowed nervously. She remembered her bravado when she first met the major. Her manner, then, was abrupt and nonsensical. At the time, her temper was boiling over with thoughts of her brother and what happened to him, and she was blind to the consequences of her action. She even had the temerity to confront her prey in the security of its own den. That, though, was many months ago. Today she glanced at the document on the desk and wondered if she'd just signed away her life.

Even so, she said, 'I won't change my mind, sir.'

'Good. *Scientia potentia est* to quote our mutual friend.' The major, using his feet, shuffled his golf balls back into a line.

'What does that mean, sir?' she asked.

'*Knowledge is power*, as Mycroft Holmes will tell you. It's what we do here.'

With that, he reached out and pulled the communication cord, then went back to his golf practice, ignoring her. Mary fidgeted anxiously from one foot to the next. A minute later, there was a knock on the door, and when he shouted 'Enter', Tiggs came in.

'Tiggs, there you are. Take Miss Finch to Mr Frobisher's haunts. He has a new pupil. Afterwards, give her the Cook's tour. There's a good lad.'

'Yes, sir,' Tiggs said. 'This way, miss,' and he indicated they should leave.

As Mary turned to follow, the major gave a slight cough to get her attention.

'We are unusual. The opportunities we offer the fairer sex would be seen as most remarkable outside these walls. You are young and you have potential. That is what we are investing in. So, do not let me down, Miss Finch. And remember: we are a family. Please do not forget that.'

Tiggs closed the door behind them and with a skip, walked ahead of Mary.

'Blooming queer family, miss,' he smirked and winked over his shoulder at her. 'I mean, you'd want him as a dad?' Mary grinned with relief. 'I'm Tiggs, by the way, but you can call me Tommy.' He held out his hand but kept walking. 'You want to know something, you come to me—I knows everything there is to know about here, and I'll see you right.'

Mary shook his hand.

'What do you do here, Tommy?' she asked.

''Ere,' he tapped his nose and mocked a serious look. Then, imitating the major, said, 'You don't ask questions like that—that's a secret.' He sniggered, and, looking around him, whispered, 'I just work at the front desk at the moment, with our watchman—that's George. But just you see…' He grinned. 'I'll be with the big boys one day.' He pointed his fingers like gun barrels and fired them down and along the corridor, making the appropriate sound of pistol shots. Mary grinned back.

'Who's this Mr Frobisher bloke I'm seeing… I mean, where… I mean…' Mary stuttered.

'Yeah, confusing ain't it?' Tommy laughed. 'Well, all I can say is you're in for it if you're seeing *the Prof* first before anything else. That's the lion's mouth for sure, and make no mistake.' He appeared very impressed.

'The Prof?' Mary asked.

'The professor. A brain box! Head's as big as a pumpkin.'

Mary rubbed her neck and bit her lip. She continued to wonder just what she'd gotten herself into.

Tommy led her down the stairs and into the basement. Down there it seemed considerably colder than the rest of the building, even colder than outside. They walked along a bare brick corridor, towards a single door at the end, the only door to be seen. An electrical cord ran along the ceiling that lit two faint bulbs hanging loosely from them. The corridor was bare of anything else. Their footsteps echoed. From being hot and uncomfortable, she shivered and drew her coat tighter around her shoulders.

Tommy knocked on the door, waited a few seconds, and then entered. He was about to introduce Mary when the man seated in the corner rose and said, 'Ah! You must be Miss Finch. I am expecting you. Come in, Miss Finch. Tiggs, you may go.' He waited until the boy left, then gave Mary a deep, penetrating stare. 'I do not tolerate fools, Miss Finch. You are not a fool, I take it.'

'I should hope not, sir,' Mary said.

The man grumbled. 'Hope is for fools,' he muttered loudly enough for Mary to hear.

No longer feeling cold, Mary felt hot again.

THE TESTS

THE MAN, Frobisher, was tall and gaunt, balding, aged in his fifties, with a pockmarked face. It was the face of someone who'd contracted smallpox and survived. His head was of normal size, not as big as a pumpkin. He wore ill-fitting and deeply creased clothes that hung off him in an ungainly fashion. He did not wear a wedding band, and Mary assumed he was either unconcerned about his appearance or had a less-than-caring landlady looking after him because he also wore one black and one blue pair of socks and shoes that needed polishing. Sniffing quite unpleasantly, he walked to a blackboard against a wall and slapped it with the back of his hand.

'What is missing?' he asked.

'Sir?'

'Do not 'sir' me, young lady,' he said sharply, and Mary jumped. 'What is missing?'

On the blackboard were written a series of numbers in a very small handwriting.

25, 100, 64, 16, 81, 36, 9.

Frobisher took out a stopwatch and set it in motion. He was waiting patiently. Mary broke out in a sweat, and she chewed her very dry lips nervously.

Before many seconds passed, she said, 'F-f-forty-nine, sir.' At the same moment, he clicked the watch and gazed at where the hand stopped.

'Because?'

'The numbers are all squares,' she said matter-of-factly. 'Three times three equals nine, four times four equals sixteen, five times five is twenty-five, and so on. The missing one is seven times seven… forty-nine,' her voice trailed off into silence.

Frobisher gazed at her through narrowed eyes.

'So, you have a rudimentary knowledge of mathematics,' he said, a little unimpressed if anything, and curled his fingers at her. 'Come.'

He led Mary to a table with various objects on it.

'Look!' He washed a hand over the top of them. Grasping a large cloth resting on the back of a chair, he threw it across the objects, completely covering them. 'Now, list what was on the table,' he said.

A knot tightened Mary's stomach. She'd not expected this. Like the numbers, this was a test. She closed her eyes and shuffled anxiously. She was feeling hot again, fully aware, even with her eyes closed, that he was looking at her intently.

'A l-l-lady's fan …'

'It would hardly be a man's. Colour?'

Mary smiled sheepishly and started to blush.

'Blue… A silver snuff box… A paperknife… A book—'

'Title?'

'A… a… dictionary… I think… Brown cover… Oxford Dictionary… A butterfly? Yes, a butterfly pinned to a card! A fountain pen… with the lid off… Cigarettes—'

'How many?'

'Ahem… five, no, six, no five… five… I think. Buttons. I'm not sure how many. And a funny square silver box, and… and I don't know what it is, but it's not another snuff box…'

Mary swallowed. She was sure there were other objects, but what they were…

Frobisher exhaled loudly and once more pursed his lips, this time tighter.

'Is that it?' he asked after a few moments of silence.

Mary glanced up at him and bit her lip to say that's all she remembered.

'The coins? Did you not notice them? What about the ring—gold with a diamond?'

Mary shook her head slowly. 'No, sir. I'm sorry, I didn't...'

He turned away.

'Nor the baby mittens, I suppose,' he muttered as if disappointed. 'The metal box is a cigarette lighter. There were five cigarettes. One had been smoked and was half the length of the others. There were four buttons: two black, two brown.'

He went back to his desk, took out a sheet of paper, and began scribbling. Sitting hunched as if some ailment of posture troubled him, he seemed to be ignoring Mary.

She, on the other hand, looked at him curiously, noticing his small handwriting, how his face was quite near the paper as he scribbled, and, like most left-handers, his wrist bent at a crooked angle as he wrote. The thought that she'd failed his test sat prominently in her mind. Inwardly, she despaired. She was barely through the door... She took a deep, silent breath, and, waiting on his pronouncement on her future, glanced around.

The room, and she understood that this was *his* room, was bare of furniture. There was the desk where Frobisher sat, the table that had the objects, and a chair beside it. There was the bookcase, the blackboard, and the sink with a mirror. Beside the sink, on a small table, were a spirit stove and a kettle. Various tins nearby, along with a half-empty bottle of milk, suggested tea. Electric lights lit the room.

Several bulbs gave an even spread. There were no windows. A portrait of a very young Queen Victoria hung from a wall. On a coat stand near the door was a dark mackintosh, totally unsuited for the cold weather, a large woollen scarf, and a dark jacket, hat and umbrella. The only other objects were resting on the desk where Frobisher worked.

Without looking up from his writing, Frobisher said, 'My bookcase. Tell me something odd about it.' He waved a hand imperiously, shooing her towards it.

Mary wandered over to the bookcase at the far end of the room. It contained a variety of volumes, on a wide variety of topics—science, mathematics, natural history, some novels, a bible, reference books, medical books, all in no particular order on the two shelves. She ran her fingers idly across the spines. She took some out and checked if they were indeed books, and not some cleverly prepared facsimile. They were books, and there was nothing particularly odd about them.

'Well?' he asked irritably. He'd not take his eyes off the note he was scribbling.

Determined not to be hurried, Mary took her time surveying the contents once more, all the while aware of his impatience. There was still nothing odd about the books, except…

'I'm not sure, sir… but the only thing… well, it's not strange… but… well, not even odd… but…'

'Stop procrastinating,' he grunted brusquely.

'Well, sir, they are all single books, I mean single copies, except there's two copies of *Jane Eyre*.'

'Are you sure?'

'Yes, sir.'

'Are they the same?'

Mary took both books; they had been placed on separate shelves. As far as she could tell, they were exactly the same.

'Check the editions,' he said sardonically, waggling his pen at her.

Mary opened the books and scanned the flysheet.

'Yes, sir, they are the same.'

'Take one and keep it safe. You have other books in your rooms?'

'Not really, sir.'

'Then get some, but never two that are the same, is that clear? And none that are new. They must all be old and well thumbed. And you are to place that one amongst them—it must not look out of place. You are to read the book, become familiar with it. It will be your favourite book from now on. Is that clear?'

Mary nodded even though it wasn't.

He finished his note, sealed it in an envelope and held it out towards her.

'Give this to Major Carshaw.' Mary took the envelope. Frobisher quickly jotted down another note and folded it in half. 'And take this to Tiggs. It entitles you to receive ten pounds. With it you will purchase the books. Give the boy the receipts for them.'

'How many books, sir?'

'You have ten pounds,' he said, as if speaking to a child. 'Go to the Charing Cross Road. You will find many second-hand bookstores there.'

With that, the man resumed his seat and, whatever he was doing before Mary had entered, he continued doing. Mary waited uneasily, unsure of just what had happened. Then, understanding he'd ended the interview, she edged nervously to the door.

'Is… that it, sir?' she asked.

'Be here tomorrow at nine. Bring lunch and your brain. You can find your own way out, I suppose.'

He flicked his hand, dismissing her.

6

TO BAKER STREET AND BACK

MARY GAVE Mr Frobisher's note to the major. He read it and made no comment. He merely nodded. The note, like her letter of introduction, ended up in the grate. By contrast, when she gave *the Prof's* chit to Tommy Tiggs, the boy's eyes, blue as robins' eggs, bulged, then narrowed suspiciously as his brows furrowed. He whispered, 'Ten pounds? 'Ere, how many did you remember?'

Mary whispered back, 'Nine.'

Tommy's mouth dropped open.

'Blimey!' he said softly. 'Two… and one of them I guessed! And the missing number?'

'Forty-nine.'

'And the bookcase thing?'

Mary held up a copy of *Jane Eyre*.

'Blimey!' he whispered again, clearly impressed. He

rushed off, coming back a few minutes later with ten sovereigns.

After placing the money in her purse, the doorman gave her an envelope that was resting in a tray beside him.

'From Mr Frobisher—'

'From *the Prof?*' Tommy said. He stared startled at the envelope. His mouth opened in awe, only to shut tightly when the doorman muttered and gave him a deep glare of annoyance.

'The note is to be read this evening,' the doorman said. '*This evening,* not before,' he emphasised.

Mary pocketed the note.

Before she left, Tommy quickly showed her around the building, pointing out some of the more important rooms, but not explaining in any detail what happened behind their closed doors. She suspected that he didn't know, he merely acted knowledgeably. Nevertheless, she enjoyed the *Cook's* tour, mainly because of Tommy's enthusiasm—he obviously loved his job.

With that done, Mary could finally leave.

Once outside, she took a deep breath of relief. It was a pleasure to be in the open again. The cold air felt refreshing, and her face soon cooled. She was unsure of how well she'd done. No letters of recommendation were requested, no one said she was even employed, no confirmation whatsoever was given; instead she was handed ten pounds and told to return in the morning. She'd passed whatever test was given, or so she assumed—and judging by Tommy's reaction, she'd passed it well.

Elated by her success, her mind reeling and her feet unable to keep still, Mary walked with a spring in her steps to the Charing Cross Road. She visited several second-hand book stores and purchased ten books. There must be a reason for being asked to do this, but whatever that was, it eluded her. She chose the books carefully: all old and well used, and all novels, innately understanding that the books ought to be of the sort she'd read, and not manuals or medical or legal volumes. Weighed down by her purchases, she'd been over enthusiastic and bought almost more than she could carry, Mary caught the omnibus to Baker Street. Nevertheless, she was looking forward to reading them. That at least was a bonus.

Mary arrived in time to see a carriage pull away from 221B. She briefly glimpsed the lone occupant. Mr Sherlock Holmes sat with his back against the seat, his palms upwards, fingers twined together in a cat's cradle. He was gazing at his hands with a meditative look, and he didn't notice her waving.

To her surprise, the Dibble's pie shop was closed. Through the window, she could see her friend, Archie, scrubbing a table top with a dishcloth while whistling. Mary knocked on the glass. Archie smiled and opened the door.

'Closed?' she asked.

Archie took a deep breath and nodded. ''Fraid so.' He threw the cloth into a bucket beside the table.

In a corner sat Sally Dibble, who everyone called Sossie. The ten-year-old was moping. She kicked her feet and scowled as if to herself. Archie, seeing Mary watching, shook his head as if to say, *don't ask.*

'Where's grandpa?' Mary enquired. He would normally be behind the counter, serving.

'In the nick!' Archie said.

'What? Arrested? Archie—'

'Nah! Giving a statement with grandma.' Archie grinned broadly. 'We got burgled this morning.' He flicked his chin towards Sossie.

'It wasn't *my* fault.' The girl grunted, pouted, folded her arms and stared back defiantly.

''Ere, what's going on?' Mary asked.

'A thief came in through the storeroom window, the one that was your bedroom,' Archie said.

'But you nailed the window shut after Black Bob broke in,' Mary said, remembering an incident that happened earlier in the year.

'And little miss helpful there removed the nails some months back and didn't tell me,' he said looking at his sister.

'There was a smell in the room, and it needed airing. That's what grandma said.' Sally huffed at Archie.

'She didn't say for you to pull up the nails, did she?'

'How was I to know?' Sally grunted again and swung

herself off the chair and marched out of the room. Once on the stairs, she thumped her feet heavily on each tread as she climbed them.

'Stamp harder,' Archie shouted. 'I reckon they ain't heard you in Buck House yet.' The door to Sossie's bedroom slammed. He shook his head. 'The *House Breaker* stole a few quid grandpa had lying about, grandma's best knife and me gloves.'

'Gloves?'

'Yes, my new gloves! Well, one glove, actually. What's the use of one glove to anyone?'

'A one-handed man,' Mary suggested impishly.

Archie huffed, not amused. 'Worse still, he got away with grandma's wedding ring. She don't wear it anymore on account of all the work she does—pulling it off, putting it on again.' He exhaled deeply. 'Seen that?' He flicked his eyes at the newspaper on the table.

Mary picked up the paper. It was the same edition that the doorman at Deacon House had.

'Milverton? Yes. Murdered.'

'One of his victims, you reckon?'

'Wouldn't surprise me in the least.' Mary sniffed and pushed the paper away. She remembered the man sitting pompously in his carriage that day she became maid to Mrs Grady. 'That smile of his. Still makes me shiver.'

'He had it coming to him,' Archie said dismissively. 'My manners! Well, what happened? How did your first day go? You're out early?'

'Well…' Mary hesitated, still unsure of how well she'd done and what she should, or could, say—she recalled the paper she'd signed. 'All right, I suppose. I'm to start properly tomorrow. But the people are strange. All except young Tommy. He seems a good sort.'

'And these?' Archie tapped the pile of books.

'Reckon I'm gonna have a lot of time on my hands in the evenings,' Mary said. She shied away from looking at him directly. 'So, what better opportunity than this to better myself.'

They settled down and talked. After a while, grandpa and grandma returned, saying that the police held out little hope of finding the thief. Grandma's ring was their best chance of finding him, as it was distinctive and would probably be pawned for cash.

After eating, Mary headed off home, agreeing to meet everyone again on Sunday—the Salvation Army choir was performing carols in Trafalgar Square.

On her way, Mary bought something for tea and for the next morning's breakfast. Climbing the stairs to her room, she fiddled with her keys. The house was quiet. She peered along the landing below hers, to the bathroom that she and the occupants of that floor shared, and down the stairwell, from where musty smells arose. No one was about; there was not a sound to be heard.

She gave a silent groan. Her bedsitting room was dark and miserable and deeply unwelcoming. In Mrs Grady's house she had Cook, Mr Venables, Ella, Fortune and even Mrs Grady she could talk to, not to mention the gardener and the occasional daily help who came along. She even knew the postman, the butcher's boy, who delivered weekly, and the milkman. Here, she knew no one.

She lit a fire and sat beside it until she warmed up. Then she unpacked her books and managed to fill most of one shelf. Her copy of *Jane Eyre* was slipped in amongst them.

As some money remained from the ten pounds, she would go to the market near the Elephant and Castle, and the nearby Old Kent Road had lots of second-hand shops.

It worried her that she'd not told Archie what she was doing. There was a time, and not so long ago, when she would have told him everything. Now she couldn't. Was this how her life would be from now on? Evasion and lies? There was a price to pay for working for the major —Mary had no doubts about that now.

Wanting something to do, she dusted and tidied the flat. When she finished, she peered out of the window— tiny people navigated the pavements below. She listened carefully. The sounds from the street were mere whispers. The house, taller than the surrounding ones, meant she could see across roofs and chimney pots, all the way across London in a northerly direction towards the river. It was a smoky view of greys and blues.

By early evening, remembering the envelope given to her, Mary opened it. It contained a single sheet of paper, with numbers written on it in Mr Frobisher's neat, but tiny handwriting.

40-2-42, 296-2-32, 2-6-14, 56-11-27

Mary looked at it puzzled. She turned it over. The back was blank. She lifted it up to the light. There was nothing to see of any interest. She checked inside the envelope. It was empty. For several minutes Mary stared at the numbers. They must mean something, why else give it to her? She spent several minutes considering them, even turning the sheet upside down and back-to-front against the light, to see if that made sense of it. Shrugging, she placed the paper onto the table.

After a late tea, she pulled the curtains, ready for bed. It was pitch black outside. Mary set her alarm, changed, and got into bed to keep warm, allowing the fire to die in the grate. She read a little from the Penny Dreadful she bought and was about to blow out her lamp when she paused. She looked up at the ceiling, closed her eyes in concentration, drummed her fingers against her legs and smiled. What was it she'd read? It was in a Penny Dreadful... years ago... Mary climbed out of bed, grabbed the book, *Jane Eyre*, retrieved Mr Frobisher's note, and sat back in bed. A few minutes of flicking through the book and counting, she burst out laughing and slammed it shut.

Just as she was about to extinguish the lamp, she paused once more. Crushing the note into a ball, Mary climbed out of bed and placed it into the flames of the fire. She watched as the note burned, until it was completely consumed and glowing ashes were all that remained. She set her alarm clock and turned out the lamp. Mary needed to be up and about early tomorrow.

7

A FACE FROM THE PAST

MARY AWOKE WELL before her alarm rang. Restless with anticipation and anxious to be away, she ate breakfast hurriedly before leaving. She tip-toed down the stairs, careful not to make any noise and wake the other occupants of the house.

Once outside, she rushed to the shop that was her destination, *Mr Marshall, Confectioners to the Elite*, which lay just off Oxford Street and always opened early.

The bell dinged brightly as she pushed the door. It had been many months since she was last here, and she closed her eyes and inhaled deeply. Her mouth immediately watered and a wide smile cracked her face. She was assaulted by the most glorious of sickly-sweet smells imaginable—icing and freshly baked cakes, honey, marzipan, demerara sugar, molasses, and so much more besides, a heady cocktail putting to shame the cup of tea and slice of buttered bread she'd eaten for breakfast.

She opened her eyes to the sight of jars and jars of coloured sweets populating the shelves. Layers and layers of the most delicious-looking cakes sat temptingly behind glass counters. Several oil lamps lit the room with a warm, flavoursome light that sparkled off the polished glass. Mary took another deep breath, revelling in the overpowering scent. The shop had changed little.

Even at this early hour, several people were commanding Mr and Mrs Marshall's attention. Mrs Marshall, a small, thin woman, gushed with joy as she served them, while her rotund husband, equally jovial, beamed happily. Mary leant down to get a better look at the carrot cakes, deciding which she would purchase. Snow white icing was drizzled across their tops, with the most lurid of green sugar paste moulded into leaves, and the most fluorescent of orange paste, shaped as carrots, decorating the edges.

Mary asked a shop girl to put the cake in one of their richly patterned cardboard boxes. With that done, Mary carefully placed the box inside a cloth bag she carried. When she paid, she giggled to herself, a sense of triumph made a lump in her throat. She checked the time on her watch and glimpsed the shop assistant giving her an envying look. Her heart fluttered, and she gave Mr Venables a silent thank you for his present. She'd have to hurry to get back to Whitehall and not be late.

She was just about to leave when, once more, the bell above the door dinged loudly. When she caught the reflection in one of the mirrors of who entered, she stiffened. The smile fled her face just as Mr Marshall's expression suddenly brightened. She eased around and was looking into the cold, silent eyes of James Grimwig, her former employer, a blackmailer and, she had no doubt whatsoever, a murderer.

He had not changed. His hair was still shining black and neatly combed. His face, handsome as she remembered. His dark eyes were just as penetrating. He was tanned, as if he spent many days in the sunshine, and his face and hands wore a healthy olive hue.

'Well, well, girls, look who we have here,' he said.

His daughters, the triplets, Rosamund, Leticia and Portia, who were the same age as Mary, scowled in unison, recognising their former maid. Behind them, their mother, Dora Grimwig, a pretty flaxen-haired woman with a heavily powdered face and rouged lips, coloured up angrily.

'It's been a while, Mary,' Mr Grimwig said, his voice as sickly-sweet as the cakes on display.

Mary edged sideways, nervously; her eyes fixed on the man.

'I-I thought—' she stuttered.

'That I was in Manchester?'

Mary nodded.

'Your partner, Milverton, is dead, I read,' he said. He

winked, and a smile cut across his face. 'And *all* his papers have been destroyed, it is reported.'

Mary grimaced. There was no point denying that she didn't know Milverton. Grimwig firmly believed she did and they were working together.

Grimwig had been blackmailing the Earl of Marshmere. When the letters he'd been using to do so were stolen, he blamed Mary. He accused her of stealing his wife's jewels, since he couldn't very well accuse her of stealing the letters. In order to prove her innocence, Mary had to find the thief who stole the letters. Her success in doing so nearly cost her and Archie their lives, but it was instrumental in Grimwig's downfall. Though Milverton never got the prize he wanted—the letters—she always suspected he got something, enough to make Grimwig's life uncomfortable. And perhaps that was why he'd fled London for Manchester and places abroad, to escape the attention of an even more accomplished blackmailer.

Mary sidled towards the door and the Grimwigs parted, allowing her passage between them.

'Leaving so soon?' Dora Grimwig said tartly.

'Maybe Mary could take tea with us, mother,' Portia sneered.

'Well, she has come up in the world, hasn't she?' Rosamund smiled smugly.

'From lighting the fires to making the beds, you mean?' Leticia scoffed.

'Oh, such an advancement in rank,' Rosamund said.

'Soon she won't know herself.' She and her sisters tittered.

'Yes, Jim, maybe Mary ought to take tea with us one afternoon,' Mrs Grimwig said. 'What do you think?'

'Oh, don't you worry, Dora. Mary and me will see each other again,' he said. 'By the way, how's your friend? Archie, isn't that his name?'

He opened the door for Mary. His tanned fingers were bedecked with rings. As she approached to leave, his arm shot out and grasped the opposite door frame, barring her way.

'Yes, his name is Archie,' he said. 'Archibald Dibble, of Baker Street.' Then he gazed at her, darkly, and smiled.

Mary shivered. She felt Grimwig's utter contempt, and her skin crawled. She'd gone hot and was desperate to get outside into the cold morning air and to be away from them. The law had yet to catch up with him for all his misdeeds. Now, seeing him so brazen, she wondered if indeed it would. She ducked under his arm to leave. He laughed, and his wife and daughters sniggered behind her.

Finally outside, Mary gasped for a breath then startled once more.

A large, broad-shouldered middle-aged man, standing behind the four-wheeler the Grimwigs came in, suddenly presented himself and almost blocked the pavement. He stood well over six feet, and his bulk was muscle. The carriage driver looked at him suspiciously. The man was dressed showily in a chequered suit that fitted him tightly. If anything, it appeared a size too small, making him appear even larger. A flat black cap swaddled his bald head and a red bandana was wrapped around his neck. If the various scars criss-crossing his purple face were not distinctive enough, the whole left side was tattooed with an intricate swirling pattern. He scowled and sneered and balled his hands into fists. They were like bears' paws.

There was something deeply unpleasant about him. The way he was looking at her sent a shiver up her spine. It was the same look Black Bob, a man in Grimwig's employment, had given her. He'd tried to kill her and almost succeeded.

Mary retreated slowly, wary of the man's cold, unforgiving eyes. Oddly, those eyes that were at first looking at her, and doing so intently, now they looked into the shop and seemingly towards Mr Grimwig. A dark, dangerous curiosity inhabited his gaze. It was as if he were waiting.

Mary didn't bother to find out for what. She took to her heels, her heart thumping fearfully quickly, and she ran until she found an omnibus. Climbing on board, she was grateful for the presence of the other passengers. Her legs were trembling and her mind was numb as her heart continued to pound relentlessly. The large, gruff man, filled her thoughts completely.

She was relieved when she arrived at Deacon House.

She'd raced to it as soon as she dismounted the omnibus. It felt safe to be inside. She must have looked a state; she was red and perspiring and breathless. No doubt everyone would think she'd run because she was late. She didn't say anything. Tommy let her into Mr Frobisher's basement room, informing her that the gentleman was a late riser, as if to say there was no need to rush.

'Cake?' Tommy said when he saw the box Mary brought. He gave her an inquisitive look. 'Teacher's pet, eh? Cor, wished I'd thought of that.'

Mary managed a weak smile for the boy—she was still flustered and her mind was still in Mr Marshall's shop, but she was calm enough to be able to think again.

'No,' she said. 'It's nothing like that.'

'I bet!' Tommy said, cheekily. He took a deep sniff of the box and licked his lips. 'Carrot cake! My favourite.' He lit the spirit stove and settled the kettle on it. 'It'll soon be nine,' he explained, 'and *the Prof* likes his tea in the morning.' The boy hesitated a moment, chewed his lip, and his brow crinkled. 'Listen, miss, can I ask a favour?'

'If I can help, I'll help.'

'Well, seeing as you're tight with *the Prof,* can you put in a good word for me?'

'I'd hardly say we were tight,' Mary said. She'd found a knife and was cutting the cake into triangles.

'Well, I ain't seen anyone that's done his puzzles like you, so I reckon you will be. It's just I don't want to be a doorman all me life, like George up there. I mean, Mr Bradley is a nice man… but…'

'You've got me at a disadvantage,' Mary said. 'I ain't got much of a clue about anything that happens here. Really, Tommy. Not much of a one.'

'But when you do, miss, just drop a hint… maybe ask for me help sometimes when they send you out and about.'

'Out and about?'

'Yeah, I reckon they will.'

'To where?'

'Blimey! You really don't know, do you?'

'What did I just say?'

'I thought you was practising.'

'Practising?'

'Yeah, being, well, practising being sneaky and silent and all that.'

Mary shrugged. 'Honest, Tommy, I'm just learning the ropes. Or at least I hope I will be. I'm sure I ain't passed all his tests yet.'

'Well, when you do, go on, miss, put in a word or two—'

'About what, Tiggs?' Frobisher, standing by the door, was peeling off his mackintosh.

'Mr Frobisher, sir, I was just… just…'

'Bothering Miss Finch unnecessarily?'

'No, Mr Frobisher, Tommy wasn't—'

'Cake!' Frobisher nodded approvingly, cutting Mary

short. 'So, there is a brain between those ears after all, and yesterday was not a chance.'

Tommy gawped.

'The book cipher, Tiggs,' he said as he placed his hat and umbrella on the coat stand, 'is almost impossible to crack.' He laughed softly to himself. 'Almost, but not quite.'

Beaming a smile, Mary proffered a saucer with a slice of cake to Frobisher. '*Bring Cake for Breakfast,* as asked for, sir,' she announced proudly.

'Yes, Miss Finch, if you are half as smart as you obviously think you are, you'll do nicely. *We* have much to learn. Some you will do here and some you will do at home by yourself. Oh, good morning, Tiggs.' Frobisher flicked his head towards the door for the boy to go.

Tommy shrugged and went dejectedly. Mary hurriedly followed him.

'Tommy,' she called. She handed him a slice of carrot cake on a saucer. 'Maybe we can help each other. If you see a really large man in a chequered suit, you tell me. You'll know who I mean—the left side of his face is completely tattooed.'

'What? Completely?'

Mary nodded. 'You look out for him and I'll see what I can do for you. Deal?'

The boy grinned in approval. 'Deal.' He held out his hand and shook hers. 'But who is he?'

'I don't know. Just keep an eye out for me.'

Her anxiety returned. She could see the man as he watched her go, just the same way the murderer, Black Bob, watched her when she was almost run down by a hansom—at the time Grimwig and Boots were trying to scare her. She remembered that Bob followed her and Archie to Limehouse and tried to murder them. She feared the large man might pursue her as well, and in her nervousness to get away, she'd not noticed.

❦ 8 ❦

FIRE-FISTS FURIE

IT SEEMED like it was a day for old faces. When Frobisher said, 'Let us begin,' he escorted Mary into a room somewhere at the back of the building. The room was empty of furniture except for a table and several thick mats laid in a wide square on the floor. Three women were standing on the mats, and one, with a severe face, smirked openly when she saw Mary enter.

Mary recognised her as the woman who'd followed her into Regent's Park last summer when she was hunting Mr Boots. A confrontation ensued when they met again later that evening.

'Ladies,' Frobisher said, 'this is Mary. She is new. And she brought cake!' He smiled as he placed a plate on the table. This was something special, and Mary knew that only too well, by the look of admiration on the faces of two of the women. The third woman, however, remained as severe as always, wearing the same look Mary remembered in Regent's Park. The compliment, however, made Mary blush. She wasn't used to such tributes and being placed under the spotlight.

Frobisher introduced the very unimpressed woman as Miss Danvers, their instructor.

'Clever, aren't we?' Danvers said to Mary, when Frobisher left. She pecked a piece of the cake and screwed up her face as if it was bitter. 'Never did like carrots.'

She waved Mary to stand beside the others.

'Good morning, ladies,' Danvers said. 'My job is to teach you how to look after yourselves. Ours is the weaker sex. That becomes our advantage.' She smiled and, placing the back of her hand across her forehead, pretended to swoon. Everyone giggled. 'What happens if a man grabs our arm. What are we to do? Mary, grab my arm with your right hand.'

Mary took her wrist and the woman gave a bored and theatrical sigh.

'Grab it like you mean it,' she barked. 'Tight! Hard! Grip it like you are trying to pull me along.'

Mary immediately tightened her grip. In an instant, Danvers clamped her left hand over Mary's hand, holding it tightly in place. The woman leant forward and whispered, 'You gave me a black eye that day we met. You didn't know that, did you?'

Danvers twisted the fingers of her right hand around

and on top of Mary's wrist. Her smile became a scowl and Mary screamed in pain. She tried to pull her hand away, but Danvers had a firm hold on it. Only when Mary sank to the floor in agony did she let go.

'See? How easy that was,' she said to the other women who looked on in shock. 'Up you get, Mary.' Mary arose slowly, rubbing her right arm that tingled and had gone slightly numb. She flexed her fingers and felt the tendon complain. 'Now, grab my collar as if you are pulling me towards you.' The smile returned to Danvers's face.

Even though the lesson was just an hour, it was a long hour, and afterwards, Mary ached all over. Nevertheless, she walked out of the room with her head held high, not wishing to show weakness to Danvers. But once outside, she limped unladylike up the stairs to a room where she could tidy up, and then to a room that served as a canteen.

Feeling sorry for herself and not wanting company, Mary found an empty table in a corner and very gingerly sat down. The long hour was a painful experience, especially for her bottom, which made multiple contacts with the floor. She bit her lip as she eased her weight onto the bruises that were fast developing there.

A bubble of laughter erupted from a table across the room where Danvers sat with several *older hands.* They were looking her way. One of them gave her a look of mock sympathy, as if to say, sitting must be painful. At that moment, Danvers slapped the palm of her hand hard on the table, imitating something. Their laughter erupted volcanically.

Mary's face coloured up red and she quickly looked away. Then, catching herself, she pretended to look unconcerned. She replaced her embarrassed face with the haughtiest one she could muster. If there was one thing being a maid taught her, and a scullery maid at that, it was not to show your feelings when taunted.

'That's it, miss, don't give them an inch.' The doorman eased himself down on the chair opposite her, taking Mary completely by surprise. His bulk, now that he was away from behind his desk and in the open, as it were, was considerable, and he almost entirely filled her sight. She worried about the chair he sat on, as it squeaked bitterly. 'That Danvers,' he whispered in his gruff, rasping voice, 'is a swipe-nose guttersnipe... but you'd still want her on your side if you were in a tight spot. You just wouldn't want to take her out for tea.'

Mary smiled weakly, appreciating the gentleman's humour.

'It's just that—' she started to explain only for the man to grin broadly.

'She threw you around a bit, I know.' He leant forward and whispered. 'A few months back she comes in sporting a beauty of a black eye. I'd like to have shaken the hand of him that gave her it—or hand of she that did the deed!'

The weak smile grew, and Mary felt compelled to conceal it behind her fingers. So, her encounter with Danvers was known. No doubt *her* recent encounter with Danvers was the regular *hello* she gave to the new recruits, and especially to the ones she didn't like, or those she thought were too clever. And especially to the ones who gave her a black eye.

The man handed her a cup of tea. Seeing him do so, she knew he had been waiting for her as he carried another cup for himself.

He introduced himself as George Bradley and held out his hand. Mary shook it, fearful that his grip would be excruciating as her hand vanished into his. Instead, he held her hand softly and gave it a small, friendly squeeze.

'A man with half his face tattooed, was it?' he said.

Mary huffed. She thought Tommy could keep it a secret—after all, wasn't it secrets that this place was all about.

'Don't fret, miss, or be mad with Tiggs.' Bradley had a kindly look, not unlike her policeman friend, Constable O'Connor. 'Tiggs means well. He tells me things and that's the way it should be.' He leant closer. 'Big and mean, scars and a tattoo. He still wears chequers, does he? And a red bandana?'

'You know him?' Mary asked. She drew nearer as George's voice dropped to a whisper.

'Furie. Absalon Furie. *Fire-Fists* Furie to the punters. Trouble.' George wrapped his hands around his cup of tea and the cup vanished completely, and he murmured, 'Three times bare-knuckles champion of Southern England—not that there ever was a championship.' He winked. 'An old-style leg-breaker from a family of leg-breakers.'

Mary gulped her tea. Bare-knuckle boxing was illegal. Nevertheless, when a bout took place, it drew a substantial crowd. She was once told there were few rules, and matches could last for hours. It was a bloody, serious affair. The cold finger of dread gripped Mary when she saw in her mind's eye the man's tattooed face, now knowing what he did for a living.

'So, what's he to you?' George asked. He was staring at her with a face that, while mixed with concern, was humourless.

She explained briefly how she once worked for Mr Grimwig, was wrongly accused of theft by him and had to prove her innocence. She was nearly murdered by his man, Black Bob. At the mention of the name, George Bradley nodded and gave a sardonic smile.

'Yes, I read he'd been killed. Shot by a ship's captain when he was accosting a young girl. That was you?'

Many nodded. 'Afterwards, Mr Grimwig fled London for Manchester. He thought I was working with a blackmailer, Mr Milverton. But I wasn't. Honest—'

'No one's gonna miss Milverton.' Bradley nodded his understanding. 'Except them he was filching from. I read the entire contents of his safe was found burnt to ashes in his grate. Lots of people will be heaving a sigh of relief to read that as well.'

'And none's gonna come out and say anything,' Mary said.

'Not unless they want to draw attention to themselves, and be mistaken for his killer. And now that Milverton's been murdered and all his papers destroyed, your Mr Grimwig's back.' George took in a deep breath, holding it in contemplation. 'Thinks he can take up from where he left off, does he?'

Mary's head drooped. She thought she would never have any more dealings with him again. Milverton's death changed all that.

'Well, he's gonna find that a problem.'

'Why?' Mary asked.

'There's a long line of debtors queued up waiting for Mr Grimwig. And some royal wants his guts for garters, I hear.'

'The Earl of Marshmere—he was being blackmailed by him.'

'No, not him. Countess Marshmere. She's the one with the claws.'

It was she, Dr Watson implied, who wore the pants in that relationship.

'Well, he'd better take care.' Bradley's nostrils flared. 'There are others who might take Milverton's murder as an invitation.'

'To do what?'

'Grimwig's made his fair share of enemies. Wouldn't surprise me in the least if one of them don't take matters into their own hands.'

'Murder him, you mean?' Mary's mouth dropped open. 'Like Milverton?'

Bradley nodded and slowly rose from his chair. He towered high and looked down at her from above.

'Grimwig and *Fire-Fists* Furie,' he sneered. 'Furie won't try anything in the open. He's too well-known for that. But the Imp might.' He answered Mary's curious look. 'His mate. A nasty little rat-boy he hangs with. But I thought Furie would be too proud to work for scum like Grimwig. How far the mighty have fallen.'

'How do you know him?' Mary asked.

'Did you see the scar on Furie's cheek?' George Bradley tapped the side of his face. Mary nodded—Furie had a long, prominent scar. 'I gave him that.' He winked. 'Then he broke three of my ribs.' George smiled as if it were an honour.

Mary gulped silently. George Bradley was at least the same height and build as Absalon Furie and, by his account it seemed, came out second best, and a poor one at that.

9

AN INCIDENT IN OXFORD STREET

BY THE END of the week, Mary ached all over. Miss Danvers took a certain wicked pleasure in using her to demonstrate such-and-such a hold or such-and-such a throw. During the day, any thoughts about the man Mr Bradley described as a *leg-breaker* were driven from her mind by the demands of her work. When she returned to her rooms, however, thoughts of him also returned.

Generally, though, her days in this first weeks were taken up, first by Frobisher, lecturing her about cryptology, a subject he absolutely delighted in—and as Tommy said, his head *was* as big as a pumpkin! And second, by Danvers, on the art of surveillance and self-defence. Remembering she'd not noticed Danvers following her that summer, Mary admitted, the sour faced woman was well suited to the task of tutor.

Frobisher's talks, however, were the highlight of her day, and she stayed late making notes and reading from the books he used.

Mary knew there were such things as codes, but she did not know they came in so many varieties of colours and flavours: The Caesar Shift, the Alberti's Disk, the Vigenère Square. Hieroglyphs were codes as well. You could reverse the words so her name became 'yram hcnif', or where every second letter of each word became the message—and these were the simple ones. Book ciphers, numbers instead of letters, even mirror writing, like that used by Leonardo Da Vinci—she had to be aware of them to be able to recognise them. At the end of the week, he started teaching her Morse code.

It was strange to think that a year ago, if someone told her she would become an independent woman, she'd not have believed them. Had they informed her that she, a female, would be working as—she furrowed her brow—as a what exactly she still did not quite know… Not a few months ago, she'd spoken about the *intelligence service* to Grandpa Dibble. He'd joked, calling them spies, agents, double agents, triple agents, the police and not the police at the same time. She giggled inwardly, recalling his words, because here she was, one of them—whatever one of them was.

It came as no surprise, then, that no one spoke about what they actually did. It was innately understood, or so it seemed, that whatever they did was known but never mentioned. A shiver of satisfaction washed through her—she was part of this *family*. It was that, wasn't it, the major called them? She was a female, and even so, she was trusted and relied upon; a sudden prickle of pride made her blush. How much changed in such a short time.

And she was making progress. She knew that Frobisher had a sharp tongue, and she quickly realised that the sharper it became, the more pleased he was. That Friday morning, when she solved several of his puzzles, he was particularly rude. Soon she was positively glowing with satisfaction. It was, all-in-all, with the exception of some bruises, a most rewarding week.

As she stepped out at the end of the day, a thin mist was forming. She sniffed the air and screwed up her nose in disgust. The precursor to yet another London Particular was gathering. The evening was gloomy, and with the threat of the fog, it promised to be even more so. Mary's thoughts of going home were reconsidered when she saw Tommy. Danvers suggested Mary should follow a random person and put to use what she'd been taught.

'Hello, Miss, off home?' Tommy was pulling on his gloves. He looked around, sniffed the air and scrunched up his nose. 'Miserable, ain't it?'

'Come on, Tommy,' she said. 'Let's see just how much I've learned this week.'

When she explained what she was going to do, the

boy's face brightened, and he pulled his scarf tighter around his neck. They walked to Whitehall. The pavements were busy with grey men, heads bent, wrapped up warmly, making their way home.

'Which one shall we follow?' Tommy asked.

Mary pointed to the people walking along the pavement and recited:

Eenie, Meenie, Tipsy, Toe;

Olla Bolla Domino,

Okka, Pokka Dominocha,

Hy! Pon! Tush!

Tommy burst out laughing, and Mary joined him.

She ended up pointing to a man in a sober black overcoat, carrying an umbrella and wearing a black Homburg hat.

'Come on, we'll take it in turns. You hang back a bit, and when I wave, you get ahead of me and I'll drop back a bit.'

'One of us should be on the other side of the road at times, Miss.'

'Good idea. Just make sure we don't lose him.'

'Or him sees us.'

The man walked at a pace down Whitehall, past Nelson's column, and into Charing Cross Road. Mary and Tommy followed doggedly, each taking turns leading and falling back. In the short distance, the fog become thicker. Even so, it was still clear enough for them to see.

The man slipped into Soho, weaved through several streets, and then turned into Oxford Street. There, he slowed and spent some time looking at the festive displays in some of the shop windows. He entered a small toyshop, and ten minutes later emerged carrying a parcel wrapped in richly patterned paper.

'Christmas present, I reckon, Miss,' Tommy said.

'You reckon?' A smile cut Mary's face that caused Tommy to grin sheepishly.

'He's off again,' Tommy said. 'I reckon he's a villain, Miss. A robber. What do you say?' He gave her a mischievous wink.

'Maybe he's an anarchist. I know all about them.'

'Maybe it's a bomb he's carrying, wrapped as a Christmas present. Blimey, Miss, he's gonna give it to the prime minister and *Boom*! Everyone's dead in 10 Downing Street.'

The man, his head down, weaved through the crowds and bumped into another. He apologised and tipped his hat.

'Miss! That's his accomplice. Did you see the sign he gave him?'

'We've got a right one here, Tommy.'

'The major is bound to promote me now.'

'Come on, Captain Tiggs, he's getting away.'

Laughing, they followed him down Oxford Street, where occasionally he stopped and peered through store windows along the way. He slipped into a shop, and Mary and Tommy followed him discreetly up a long and crowded stairwell. Then he seemed to change his mind. He dipped his hand inside his pocket, withdrew a few coins, and turned to head back down the stairs again. Mary, determined to follow, started after him.

'Blimey, Miss,' Tommy said. 'Look at the time. Mum will be having kittens—she expected me a quarter-hour ago.'

'Go on then,' Mary said. 'I'll catch you Monday and tell you where our assassin got to.'

Just as Tommy turned, Mary felt it. An unmistakable and firm barge. In an instant, she was lifted off the ground and propelled down the stairs. She screamed as she flew past and crashed into the people coming up the stairs. Immediately, she and those she collided with were surrounded by a crowd, anxious to see how they were. Mary sat stunned. She glanced behind her and up the stairs. She could see nothing. Whoever pushed her was gone.

Standing gingerly, she started to apologise to those she hurt, helping them up and brushing them down. She ran her fingers through her hair. This wasn't an accident, though it bore all the hallmarks of one. She could've easily lost her footing. Except, she was pushed. She struggled past the crowds and into Oxford Street. Outside, it was dark and busy. She leant against a shop window to get her breath back.

At that moment, Tommy appeared. His face was white and his eyes were staring.

'It was him,' he said hoarsely. 'The man with the tattoos.'

'Him? He pushed me?'

Tommy shook his head.

'No, another man tried to kill you. A small, dirty man. I chased after him and he went down a flight of stairs at the back of the shop.' He glanced nervously over his shoulder. 'He was in the alley, Miss, the man with the tattoos.' The boy was trembling.

'What is it, Tommy?' she asked. She held his hands to steady him. His palms were moist and his breathing was sharp.

'He was thumping seven bells out of another man.' He looked over his shoulder as a choir of police whistles sounded nearby.

'The man who pushed me?'

'Not him, no—he was looking on while the big man did it. Then they saw me. Blimey, Miss, I wasn't gonna hang around. He was big as tram.'

Mary swallowed and clenched her jaws tightly. She twitched nervously, as a policeman rushed towards the alley Tommy spoke about.

'He won't be hanging around, not with the coppers about,' she said in relief.

'I don't get it,' Tommy said. Again, he glanced around as if expecting to see the tattooed man. 'I mean, if

I was gonna do you in, not that I would, Miss, I mean, *if* I was, I wouldn't push you down some stairs. I'd push you in front of a carriage…'

Mary rubbed her neck, which was aching from her tumble. Surely, he knew he'd be pushing her into a crowd and they'd break her fall, or at least prevent a worse accident from happening. The chance of killing her, while a possibility, was, nevertheless, remote.

'It's too exposed out here and he might be seen easily if he tries it again,' she said, not quite believing it. 'There's too many people out here.'

'There were a lot inside, as well, Miss,' Tommy said.

Mary nodded. He was right, of course.

'But, Miss, why would someone want to do you in?'

She looked around, expecting to see Mr Grimwig somewhere in the crowd. The truth dawned on her. While they were playfully following someone, Mr Grimwig's man was menacingly following them, specifically her. It couldn't be a coincidence—he must have followed her from where she worked. So, not only did Grimwig know where she worked, but by now, no doubt, he also knew where she lived.

Mary looked around nervously. Absalon Furie, a man as big as a tram, would be easily spotted. His impish friend, his ratty friend, according to Mr Bradley, the one who'd pushed her, was another thing. She spotted several people hurrying to and fro, who could match the impish man's description. She briefly considered heading back to

Lambeth and her rooms when she noticed that her blouse was torn along the waist. Not only that, but her undergarment beneath the blouse was also torn. Then she noticed the blood. Examining the torn edges, she realised they were slashes. Whoever pushed her also tried to stab her.

10

AT THE DIBBLE'S PIE SHOP

TOMMY'S FACE blanched when he realised what occurred. He insisted on escorting her home. Mary decided, instead, to go to the Dibbles. She didn't want to be alone, and they'd put her up for the night.

Frightened and apprehensive, and keeping a wary eye, Mary and Tommy walked quickly down Oxford Street. Once they reached the turnoff to Baker Street, Mary said, 'Go on, Tommy, you be off home. My friends are just down there, and your mum will be worried.'

'Are you sure?' he asked.

Mary nodded. 'It's just a little way along and trust me, I ain't gonna hang about.'

Clearly upset at having to do so, Tommy reluctantly left her. Mary didn't hesitate, she walked quickly to the Dibble's pie shop.

At this late hour, the shop was dark. Lights, though,

burned in the windows above. She knocked and waited. The Dibbles were always glad to see her, ever since she first met them, several years ago. On that occasion she'd stolen one of grandma's pies because she was so hungry.

'You're early—it's only Friday,' Archie said as he opened the door.

Mary had forgotten. She'd planned to see them on Sunday. Together with Archie and his sisters, Sossie and Dot, they were going to Trafalgar Square, where the Salvation Army's choir was to sing carols. Her young friends from the Rose Garden, Mrs Grady's house in Holland Park, Fortune, Kitty and Ella, would come as well. Mrs Grady, Cook and Mr Venables all declined. Emma Watkins, someone whom she worked with when employed by the Grimwigs, would also be there. Emma had only recently become engaged, and she'd bring her fiancé, Sydney Bottle.

Mary took one last glance behind her before she entered the pie shop. The streets were dark, and the fog was still just a thin grey mist. She could see no one, at least none who looked suspicious.

'Can I spend the night?' she asked as she squeezed past Archie.

'Need you ask?' he said as he bolted the door behind her.

Mary trudged upstairs to the small sitting room, where a welcoming fire blazed. She held out her hands to warm them.

'What's up?' Archie asked. 'You look like you've seen a ghost.'

'Ghosts,' she said. 'The Grimwigs.'

'The Grim–'

'Tuesday, at Mr Marshall's sweet shop. Him, his wife and the triplets—'

'Is that blood?' He narrowed his eyes, looking at the blossom of a red stain on her blouse.

Before she could answer, the door burst open, and Archie's little sisters tumbled in. 'Mary, Mary,' Dot and Sossie shouted together, and started pulling her towards their bedroom.

'Come and see what Archie bought us,' Dot said.

'I've got shoes. Not one of Dot's hand-me downs,' Sossie said happily.

'I got a brand-new dress,' Dot said enthusiastically.

'Here, you two, give the girl a chance; she's only just come,' Archie said.

Dot and Sossie continued to pull her along.

'Girls, can I see them later? Please,' Mary pleaded. 'I'm just a bit tired—'

'Leave her alone, you two. Can't you see she's knack-ered?' Archie's brotherly growl caused Sossie to screw up her nose and Dot to harrumph at him.

'I'll come late. Promise,' Mary said.

'Helped out the gardener at Mrs Grady's house since he's poorly,' Archie explained. 'She insisted on paying me. Overpaid, as usual, and wouldn't take the difference back. I thought I'd give the girls early Christmas presents. OK. Now. What's up?' he asked.

Mary gave a feeble smile. She gingerly lifted up a corner of her blouse, where there was a slight dribble of blood. She squeezed the cut and held it tight. Archie gave her a handkerchief along with a curious stare.

Noticing Dot and Sossie were watching, Archie said, 'Go on you two, and get Mary something to eat.' Before Mary could say anything, Dot and Sossie rushed off. 'Bloomin' hurricanes, aren't they?' Archie laughed. 'Let me get some water and sort this out. Then you can tell me what happened.'

He came back with a bowl of water, and Mary dabbed the cut clean. It was small and neat, and already closed.

'He tried to kill me,' Mary said.

'Who did? Grimwig?'

Mary sighed. 'One of his men. Pushed me down some stairs—well, maybe not trying to kill me, but—'

'But cut you and pushed you.' He huffed. 'Not tried? Don't give me that. You all right, otherwise?'

'Just a few bruises. Not that you'd notice new ones.'

'Sorry? What…?'

Mary shook her head. She'd been so happy when she left Deacon House with Tommy Tiggs following the man. She was rather looking forward to showing Archie some of the holds and throws Miss Danvers had taught her. She could imagine her friend's surprise that she, a good few stones lighter, could manage to throw him so easily. Now she was deflated and sat slumped looking at the fire.

'Nothing,' she said. Instead, she explained what happened when she saw the Grimwigs, how the tattooed man was also there, and then what occurred at the store. She explained she was Christmas shopping and left it at that. It was a comfortable enough lie since she couldn't explain why she was really there.

'*Fire-Fists* Furie.' Archie exhaled loudly, recognising Mary's description.

'You know him?'

'Oh, yes,' he said excitedly, then, catching himself, he reached out and squeezed Mary's arm sympathetically. 'A couple of years back, he went toe-to-toe with the *Brentwood Butcher,* George Bradley. Forty rounds, it was. I thought Bradley was going to win, then Furie got his second wind and thumped him. I've never seen anything like it before. Bradley was a mess afterwards. But it wasn't Furie that pushed you, was it?'

Mary shook her head. 'No. If he did, I'd been clear across the street. It was his mate. Tommy saw him.' She gave the description Mr Bradley gave her of the Imp, but didn't say that the man who told her it was the *Brentwood Butcher.*

Archie nodded knowingly. 'There was a small man in Furie's corner. Sounds like him your Tommy saw. Two different people you couldn't wish for.'

'There'll be no point telling the coppers,' she said. 'It looked like I lost my footing and fell.'

'An accident, like you was clumsy and cut yourself in the process. You're sure it was the Grimwig's doing?'

'Who else? What am I going to do, Archie?'

'Maybe see Mr Holmes, he'll know what to do. But I think you're right—he was probably trying to scare you. Pushing you down those stairs wouldn't have killed you.'

'And the slash?'

Archie hunched and shook his head.

'You're not much help,' Mary moaned. 'I'm gonna have to tell the major and see if he can do something.'

'Carshaw? The one we met in the summer?'

Mary bit her lip. She couldn't explain it, at least not to Archie. Mr Holmes, though, would be a different matter. She silently cursed all this secrecy stuff once again.

'Sit there,' Archie said, 'and I'll see what's keeping them girls. Probably preparing a banquet, knowing them. If they ain't arguing first.'

Mary's eyes dropped.

'Cheer up,' Archie said. 'You're safe here. Sleep on the couch tonight. I'll get some blankets. It's a good deal warmer in here than the storeroom. Then tomorrow we'll go and see Mr Holmes.'

'Thanks, Archie.'

They talked as she ate and afterwards, she felt better.

She sat back, finally comfortable and warm, finally able to relax.

'Blimey! Potatoes for brains,' Archie said and handed her an envelope that was on the mantlepiece. It had her name printed on it by a type writer. 'I almost forgot. Found it slipped under the door this morning. I was going to give it you when you came around Sunday.'

Mary tore open the envelope and pulled out two tickets for the pantomime, *Robinson Crusoe*, at the Theatre Royal in Drury Lane. Puzzled, she turned the envelope upside down and found it was empty.

'Secret admirer, eh?' Archie nudged her in the rib.

She gruffed. 'He's done this to me before,' she said. 'Another one of his tests.'

'Who has? What test?'

'It's meant to mean something. It's just I'm too tired to think what.' Archie screwed up his eyes as if to say, *what are you talking about?* 'Just one of my bosses at work—' Mary shrugged wearily. 'Don't ask.'

'Well, if you need to take someone… there's two tickets…'

'Consider yourself asked!'

'Best suit time, I think,' Archie said. 'Your colour's back.' He nodded his approval.

Before bed, Mary saw the presents Archie bought for the girls, and then, having said her goodnights to everyone, she settled down on the couch. The glow of the fire provided a welcoming light and a soothing warmth. Tired, she yawned and slipped quietly into sleep.

How long passed, she didn't know. She was awoken by the sounds of violent knocking on the door below. Loud voices were shouting. Archie's voice boomed above them. 'Hold your horses, I'm coming.' She arose, put on one of Grandma Dibble's dressing gowns, and went to investigate.

Several policemen pushed their way into the shop. One held Archie's arm. An inspector, or so she assumed him to be, a stout, robust man with a puffy red face, was handing a piece of paper to Grandpa Dibble. Beside them, grandma was trying to speak to him.

'A warrant to search the premises,' he said. 'So, we'd appreciate everyone keeping out of our way.'

'What you talking about?' Archie yelled.

'A warrant for what?' Mary shouted.

'You'll find out soon enough,' said a plain-clothed policeman with heavy bushy eyebrows, standing by the inspector. Carrying a sense of importance, he advanced and pushed past Mary, heading up the stairs to the storeroom. He held a small jemmy in his hand. A constable came with him, and the policeman turned and placed a hand on his chest.

'Stay here, Findlay, one man's enough for this.' He nodded towards Mary. 'Keep an eye on her.'

'Oi! What's going on?' Mary asked.

He didn't answer, but carried on past her. Sossie and

Dot, awoken by the commotion, were watching with open mouths. Mary pulled them closer and out of the way.

The noise of boxes and furniture being moved and thrown about came from the storeroom. Archie struggled with the man holding him, to no avail—the inspector held his other arm. A few minutes passed, when suddenly the plain-clothed policeman burst out of the storeroom and back into the shop. His face beamed triumphantly. He held aloft a cloth sack to show the inspector.

'It's there, Sergeant?' the inspector asked.

'Knife and loot,' he said. He shook the bag and it jangled.

'Archibald Socrates Dibble,' the inspector said solemnly. 'I am arresting you for the murder of Janusz Zielinski of Knightsbridge.'

'Janusz who?' Archie said.

'I hope you know a good lawyer,' the inspector said, 'because you're going to need one.' He flicked his head to the bag his sergeant carried.

II

INSPECTOR BAYNES

MARY RUSHED UP to the inspector, demanding to know what murder? Where? How? When? And was waved away. She watched in horror as Archie was handcuffed and bundled ungraciously into a Black Maria waiting by the pie shop.

'Mary,' Archie shouted, 'I don't know what they're talking about.'

'Can't you see it's a mistake,' Mary harangued the inspector and started to tug at his sleeve to get his full attention, just as the carriage driver snapped a whip and the horses stumbled away.

'Mary, I swear, I ain't murdered no one,' Archie cried. He clutched the bars of the Black Maria, a look of absolute horror on his face.

For what seemed like an eternity, Mary stared blankly as the carriage trundled along Baker Street and into the darkness. Then she gazed dumbfounded at the policemen who was smiling triumphantly, and at the inspector, who, in contrast to his men, wore a sullen, unhappy expression.

'Archie would never do a thing like that,' Grandma Dibble said to him.

The old woman looked haggard, and she trembled as grandpa held her. At the base of the stairs, Dot and Sossie were crying. They rushed up and clung on to their grandmother.

'It must be a mistake,' Mary said, and turned to speak to the inspector, but by now he was surrounded by his men. They patted him on the back and offered him their congratulations. She'd get no information from him. Instead, she ran to number 221 and started hammering on the door.

'Mr Holmes, Mr Holmes,' Mary shouted and continued to pound the door with her fists.

It seemed to take hours before she heard a crotchety woman's voice complaining to whoever was banging on her door at this early hour. A bolt drew back, the lock turned, and Mrs Hudson, wrapped in her nightgown and carrying a lamp, peered out.

'What is it?' she asked grumpily. 'You'll wake the whole street if you don't stop this noise.'

'Mrs Hudson, I must see Mr Holmes,' Mary said.

'Mary? Don't you know what time it is? Mr Holmes—'

'Mr Holmes! Mr Holmes!' Mary pushed past her and scampered up the stairs, still shouting.

'Mary Finch! Stop this minute,' Mrs Hudson shouted.

Mary rushed through the sitting room door of flat B just as Dr Watson came out of his bedroom. The doctor, wearing his dressing gown and carrying a candle, looked irritable.

'What is the reason for this commotion?' he demanded.

'Dr Watson, I must see Mr Holmes—they've arrested Archie.'

'What are you talking about? Who arrested Archie?'

'The coppers. Just now. Please, Dr Watson, let me see Mr Holmes.'

'Now, now, Mary.' He placed the candle down and took her firmly by her arm, forcing her to sit. 'Explain yourself.'

'I was going to tell her, Dr Watson—' Mrs Hudson started to say.

'Yes, of course, Mrs Hudson. Let me do it. Mary, Mr Holmes is not here.'

Mary gaped in disbelief and tried to rise, only for the doctor to prevent her.

'Mary, sit down, be calm and tell me what has happened,' he said. 'Mrs Hudson, perhaps you can make us some tea. I know it is early, but—'

'Yes, yes, Doctor,' Mrs Hudson said, with a weary resignation in her voice. 'It's not as if this is unusual.'

'Now, take a deep breath and tell me what has occurred,' he said to Mary.

Mary bit her lip and looked up pleadingly. 'They've arrested Archie. They said he's murdered someone. Where is Mr Holmes? He has to help Archie.' She spoke quickly and swallowed nervously as she clutched the doctor's arms. Her eyes flicked around the room, expecting the detective to suddenly appear.

'Holmes is away. He is in Paris on a case for the French government. I do not know when he will be back, Mary—'

'He must come back,' Mary said. She was almost in tears. 'He must! He must! He has to help Archie—'

'Mary, I cannot contact him. He is incommunicado.'

She caught her breath and sat mortified as the room went silent. She was trembling. 'But he must come back,' she whispered.

'I can send a telegram, but there is no knowing when he will receive it,' the doctor said in a soft, calming voice.

'I am sorry to hear that.' Standing at the door was the stout, puffy, red-faced police inspector. His eyes were extraordinarily bright and were almost hidden behind his heavily creased cheeks and brow.

'Dr Watson, I tried to stop him,' Mrs Hudson said exasperated. She was holding the man's arm, but obviously to no avail.

'He's the one,' Mary said. Rising, she confronted the

policeman, only for Dr Watson to place a hand on her shoulder and draw her away.

'Inspector Baynes, is it not?' the doctor said.

The man drew a slow smile across his lips. 'I see you remember me, Doctor.'

'Yes, yes. Wisteria Lodge.'

'The Tiger of San Pedro and Mr Eccles.'

'You have arrested Archie Dibble?' he asked.

The policeman nodded; the same solemn expression Mary saw him wear in the street darkened his face.

'It is all right, Mrs Hudson, the inspector and I know each other.'

Mrs Hudson harrumphed, snorted and took a deep breath. 'It's like Piccadilly Circus here at times. I swear it is.' Shaking her head, she left, muttering, 'It's not even two in the morning—'

'But I thought you were with the Surrey Constabulary,' Dr Watson said.

'I still am. However, I am on temporary secondment to the South Kensington and Westminster Division. Seems as if they wish to teach an old country dog new city tricks.' He smiled again.

'Well, they are the ones who could learn,' Dr Watson said, shaking the man's hand. 'Come in, come in, Inspector. Mary, this is Inspector Baynes. Holmes and I had the pleasure of working with him a year ago. Do you know, Mary, he matched Holmes stride for stride in the Wisteria Lodge case?'

'Oh, Doctor, please—' Baynes held up his hand and shook his head in an awkward, self-conscious way.

'No, no. Credit where it is due. Holmes was impressed. And believe me, Inspector, that is saying something.'

'Oh, I'm sure I was a tad behind Mr Holmes all the way.'

'Now, what is this all about?' Dr Watson asked.

The inspector placed the bag taken from the storeroom onto the breakfast table and carefully tipped out the content. Various gold items, bracelets and rings, fell out, along with a large kitchen knife. The blade and handle were stained with blood. Amongst the items came a bill-fold of money, fifteen or twenty or so five-pound notes, also stained red in places. Like the knife, there was evidence that they had been handled.

'We found this bag under the floorboards in the storeroom of the Dibble's place,' he said. 'The knife looks a perfect match for the one the pathologist described.' He reached inside his pocket and withdrew a glove. Some of the fingers were stained dark red. 'This was found at the scene of a crime, the murder of Janusz Zielinski, a pawnbroker in Knightsbridge. And we found this—' from his other pocket he produced the matching pair of the glove — 'in the boy's room.'

'No, wait—' Mary started to speak, only for Baynes to raise a hand to quiet her.

'You're going to tell me about the burglary,' he said

knowingly. 'Seems the Dibbles reported a break-in a week back and some items were stolen—a knife and glove and some money… allegedly. That happened near the time of the murder. The boy, apparently, has been spending freely of late—'

'He was paid for some work by Mrs Grady,' Mary said.

'Even so—'

'Surely, Inspector, this cannot be. I and any number of people, can vouch for the boy's veracity.'

'Alas, the evidence—'

'How was it you came to the Dibbles?' the doctor asked.

'Yes,' Baynes replied, taking a deep and slow breath. The smile left his face and what remained Mary could not guess. Only it seemed to trouble him. 'There's the rub. We were informed. An anonymous source said it would be in our interest to search the Dibbles' storeroom, especially under the floorboards, in connection with Zielinski's murder.'

'But, ain't it all convenient?' Mary said. 'I mean, anonymous source? The Dibbles? Under the floorboards?'

'And I suppose these items were the ones stolen from the murdered man?' Dr Watson interrupted.

Baynes nodded.

'I see,' Dr Watson mumbled.

'As I said, there lies the rub.' The policeman wore a sour expression.

'What do you mean?' asked Dr Watson. It was clear that the policeman wasn't happy, not in the least.

'The law is as tricky as herding cats.' He stopped and groaned loudly. 'The evidence is damning. But—' Baynes tightened his mouth in both annoyance and contemplation. 'I am no martinet, Doctor, you know that of me. But I have to follow the law and the course it leads.'

'The boy might hang if what you indicate is true.'

'Oh, make no mistake, Doctor Watson, the boy *will* hang on this evidence,' he said earnestly.

A wave of nausea came over Mary as she grasped the edge of the table to keep from falling. Her legs suddenly felt weak. Dr Watson held her arm.

'But he doesn't even know this man, Zielinski… I'm sure of it,' she said pleadingly.

'Mary,' Dr Watson said softly, 'believe me when I say, were I to be murdered, apart from Holmes, there is no better man I would like to investigate my demise than Inspector Baynes. He will get to the bottom of this.'

The inspector returned him a sheepish smile.

'I appreciate your confidence, Doctor. I only hoped that Mr Holmes were here so we could discuss the matter. It looks like I will have to act alone. I will give the boy the benefit of the doubt, but what latitude I give will be tempered with my superiors' wish for a speedy conviction—we can't have willy-nilly murders in the good neighbourhood of Knightsbridge, apparently.'

Slowly and deliberately, he packed each item away inside the bag, scrutinising them as he did so. At one point, he stopped and stared at the knife and then at the bundle of five-pound notes, each displaying signs of being handled by a bare hand. And then he looked at the glove. The side of his mouth twitched, and he gazed up at the ceiling.

'I seem to recall Mr Holmes wrote a monograph—' he mused.

'Which one?' Dr Watson asked. He flicked his chin to the bookcase. 'How many different types of cigar ash exists? The effects of corrosive substances on the human body? The manifestation of bruises—'

'No, no,' Baynes said, nodding to himself as he left. 'No. Something else I have in mind. I have a copy at home—'

Mary slumped into a chair. Defeated, she felt sick. Everything was a blur; the doctor's caring face, the comfortable sitting room, the chairs and the fire, and the pictures on the wall. She gazed disbelievingly at the table where a few minutes ago lay the items from the bag the police found; and even more disbelievingly at the door she knew to be Mr Holmes's room. It was not unlike what happened to her at the Grimwigs', when she was wrongfully accused of theft. She would have gone to prison then, had it not been for Archie's help.

12

A JOURNEY TO THE ROSE GARDEN

WHEN MARY RETURNED to the pie shop, grandma was seated at one of the tables. She was shaking. Grandpa, Sally and Dot huddled around her. Grandpa had his arms wrapped around them as they were crying, and he was trying, with little success, to comfort them.

Mary felt dreadful, and she could easily have joined them. Instead, she quietly closed and bolted the shop door, and took Sally and Dot upstairs to their bedroom. Tucking them into bed, she stayed a while. The girls were too upset to sleep.

'Do your best,' she said, 'and try and get some shut eye. There ain't much to be done till it's light.'

'Archie wouldn't kill anyone,' Dot said defiantly, and then started crying again.

'It's a mistake, ain't it, Mary?' Sossie sniffed.

'Of course, it is. Archie's no killer.'

She kissed them and blew out the candle.

Mary slipped quietly into the storeroom. It was a mess. Things were strewn everywhere. A section of floorboard near the window had been prised up. Curiously, no other floorboards had been lifted. The policeman knew exactly where to look.

She went downstairs to the shop. Grandpa and grandma were still there.

'What did Mr Holmes say, Mary?' Grandma asked. She was drying her tears with a handkerchief.

Instead Mary told them what the policeman had said.

'We'll get Archie the best brief, Esme,' Grandpa said. 'It's a mistake, and he'll set it right.'

'Lawyers cost money,' Grandma said. 'We'll have to mortgage up to get some to pay for one.'

'It won't come to that,' Mary said. 'In the morning, I'll go and see Mrs Grady. She'll help. I know she will.'

'We can't ask her for money,' Grandma said.

'Well, if you can't, I can! I ain't proud!' Mary said determinedly, then screwed her lips, apologetically. 'I sorry, I didn't mean it that way, grandma.'

'I know you didn't, Mary.'

'It's just I know Mrs Grady will want to help. In any case, I got money we can use.'

'Not your brother's gift.' Grandpa shook his head. 'No.'

'Look, you lot took me in when I was desperate, and you did so without a question asked.'

'And you're grateful, we know,' Grandpa said. 'But the money was given for your future, and that's the way it will stay.'

Mary was going to argue, but it was late. And anyway, there was little point until she saw Mrs Grady.

'I'll see Ella, Kitty and Fortune when I'm there. We was going to Trafalgar Square to listen to the carols, but I'll cancel it now.'

'No, take the girls,' Grandma said. She glanced up the stairs where her grandchildren slept. She grasped Mary's hand. 'It'll take their minds off things. Take them all. It'll help to have their friends around. It'll help you as well.'

Mary nodded. 'Come on, let's all get some sleep. If we can, that is.'

She lay awake for several hours before falling into a fitful sleep. It concerned her that the police knew exactly where to look to find Mr Zielinski's stolen items. Inspector Baynes claimed that an anonymous tip led him to the location. It was plain to her that Archie would never murder anyone. In which case, he'd been set up. Yet, it made no sense. Who would want to do that? Who hated him enough? Whoever it was had done an excellent job. And how that could be, further worried her.

When she awoke, she quietly got ready, and, after a quick breakfast, hurried away towards Holland Park. She was determined afterwards to go and see Archie, so she took a change of clothes for him. Grandpa said he would try to see him as well, but he feared they would not allow it until they finished questioning him.

When she arrived at the Rose Garden, Mary rang the front door bell. Since she was now an independent woman, Mrs Grady insisted she use the front door and not the servants' entrance. Kitty answered the rings, ahead of Mr Venables, who was following a good few yards behind her. The butler slowly shook his head. Kitty smiled a fawning smile, the one she was told to wear when guests came calling, and gave a pleasant curtsey, before breaking out into a fit of giggles when Mr Venables came to stand behind her.

Mary was about to compliment the girl on her smart appearance, but having worked with her for a month before leaving Mrs Grady's employment, she knew better. Getting praise was something Kitty would have to cultivate.

'She can't keep still,' Mr Venables said. 'A jack-in-the box—popping up here and then there. Go on, off with you—' He raised his hand in a mocking way, as if he was about to slap her. Kitty tried to keep a straight face, but seeing Mr Venables suddenly break out in a smile, she giggled loudly and scampered away. 'Do you know what she did the other day with the quarterly interest from her reward money? The twenty-five pounds she got for the arrest of Mr Boots that I invested for her?' Mary shook her head. 'On her day off, she bought her friends in the Irregulars a slap-up meal—and at a smart restaurant.'

Somehow, that didn't surprise Mary.

As Mary knew where she was going, Mr Venables left her alone. The house felt different. Something she couldn't quite put her finger on caused her some unease. With thoughts of Archie filling her mind, she dismissed it, thinking it was just her apprehension at work and nothing else. That, and she was still tired from having slept so little.

Mary found Mrs Grady in the morning room. She looked pale, not unlike how she looked that day, many months ago, when a ghost vexed her. But immediately the shadow passed when the old lady saw her former maid, and that gave Mary more cause for concern. Mrs Grady was extremely proficient at putting on a good face when she wanted to. However, she knew there was no point in asking what troubled her because, at times, the old lady could be as silent as a marble statue. Instead, Mary explained why she was there.

'I shall speak to this Inspector Baynes,' Mrs Grady said. 'I shall impress on him Archie's character and that he did indeed work here that day. Tell Esme Dibble that I will call to see her on Monday. And she is not to worry about any expense. This is intolerable. Kitty,' she shouted.

The young girl rushed in. 'Yes, ma'am.'

'Kitty, go to my room and fetch my writing case.'

With that Kitty ran off, and Mrs Grady sighed pleasantly. It was not in Kitty's nature to do things slowly and ladylike.

On her returned, Mrs Grady wrote a letter and handed it to Mary. Her hands shook.

'I have taken Mr Venables's advice since that affair with the Denbies and I retained the services of a solicitor on a permanent basis,' Mrs Grady said. 'This letter instructs him to work on Archie's behalf. You will see them today. Tell Archie to keep his chin up.' She took a deep breath and chewed her lip for a second. Noticing Mary watching, she gave an awkward smile. 'Oh, Katherine!' she said with a smile to Kitty, standing beside her. 'How are we going to turn you into a lady if you're always running around?' The small girl beamed happily back at her. 'Now, *walk*, and find Mr Venables for me.'

This she did until she rounded a corner, then her scampering footsteps told a different tale.

For a moment, Mary thought Mrs Grady wanted to say something to her. But, instead, the old lady told Mary she must hurry.

'Thanks ever so much, Mrs Grady,' Mary said. 'Grandma will be relieved.'

Before leaving, Mary went to the kitchen to see Ella, Fortune and Kitty and made arrangements to meet them on Sunday for the carols. When she was alone with Cook, she asked, 'What's wrong with Mrs Grady? Her hands are trembling. I didn't want to say anything in front of her—'

'Overwork. What else,' Cook huffed and went back to kneading some dough, far more energetically than was necessary. 'You know that woman as well as I. Tell her to do something and she'll do exactly the opposite. Stubborn as a mule,' she muttered.

Cook could be just as stubborn, and Mary didn't have the time to find out what it was she wasn't telling her. She caught sight of Mrs Grady speaking to Mr Venables as she left. The butler was seated beside her, taking notes as she spoke. His look was solemn as he carried out his task. Her face looked grey.

Mary found a hansom and was taken to Holborn to the offices of Mrs Grady's solicitors.

13

DRUZE, DRUZE, CORNWALLIS
& DRUZE

THE OFFICES OF DRUZE, Druze, Cornwallis and Druze occupied a whole floor of a building in Holborn, bordering Covent Garden. The elderly Mr Druze, once a fearsome barrister in his own right, the victor of many cases before retiring from the criminal courts due to ill health, now worked to instruct them instead. He scrutinised Mrs Grady's letter through a pair of spectacles he held in his hand. His thinning hair, grizzled with iron-grey, and his sunken droopy face made him look peculiarly intelligent. He wore a plain black suit devoid of frills, as was his manner, and listened, unspeaking, while Mary explained the events at the shop. Whatever he was engaged with, to Mary's surprise, he abandoned it there and then to one of his sons.

'Come, let us go see Mr Dibble,' he said. 'He will be held in Bow Street.'

It was a short distance only. They walked in utter silence. Mr Druze's face, though impassive, somehow gave the impression that the brain behind it was working feverishly. On entering the building, it was plain to see the respect with which he was held. With little fuss, Mr Druze was taken to see an official. Mary, asked to wait outside the office, was about to complain but bit her lip— Mr Druze no doubt knew his business. He certainly seemed more competent than the only other solicitor she knew—Fogarty Hawthorne—who had plagued Mrs Grady not so long ago and was now a resident of one of Her Majesty's prison.

Mr Druze grimaced with a dour expression when he emerged from the office. He narrowed his eyes and looked grim and determined.

They were taken to a room to wait. A few minutes later, Archie was escorted in. Handcuffed and still wearing his pyjamas and dressing gown, he looked drained. Mary handed her bag of Archie's clothes to a policeman, who rummaged through it, checking it thoroughly.

'There ain't no file hidden inside,' Mary huffed. He sneered and laid the clothes beside Archie. 'It'll be in the pie I bring him,' Mary muttered.

The solicitor turned his eyes onto the policeman, who took the hint and departed.

'I am Druze. Your legal representative, Mr Dibble,' he began. 'The evidence against you is compelling.'

'I didn't murder anyone,' Archie said. 'You do believe me, don't you, sir?'

'What I believe is neither relevant nor important, young man. What the jury believes is all that matters.'

Archie raked his fingers through his hair. He leant forward, almost pleading. 'But I didn't do it, sir. How can they think I'd murder anyone?'

'How do you think the murder weapon, a knife, and the stolen items, were found in your home?' Mr Druze asked.

'It's obvious, ain't it? It was when we had the break-in. It was left then.'

'A knife used in a murder, along with a bloody glove, was left to be found before the crime had been committed?'

'No, I mean… it was stolen then… and left… afterwards…' Archie stammered.

'Why would anyone want to do that?'

'I don't know… I mean… I mean…' Archie hunched.

'Janusz Zielinski. Who is he?'

'Honestly, mister, I ain't never heard of him or seen him in my life,' Archie pleaded.

'A ring. Gold. A large sapphire surrounded by several small diamonds. Engraved inside the band, *to A from E,* do you know it?'

'Sounds like grandma's wedding ring.'

'Would it surprise you to know it was found in Mr Zielinski's pawnbroker's shop?'

'Found?' Archie's brows furrowed and his mouth fell open. He went silent.

'The receipt, discovered in Mr Zielinski's books indicate a Mr Archibald Dibble pawned it,' the solicitor said.

Archie sat back and looked appalled. 'No, no, no,' he blurted. 'No, Mr Druze, no… We was burgled! Grandpa went and reported it—'

Mr Druze looked unimpressed.

'Why would he leave the ring behind if he ransacked and killed Mr Zielinski?' Mary asked.

'Be silent, Miss Finch,' Mr Druze said sharply. 'Why did you direct Miss Finch to sleep in the front room and not her usual place—the storeroom?'

Archie gaped.

'The storeroom is freezing—' Mary said and was instantly silent when the solicitor's gaze fell on her.

'Yet you did, and away from where she normally slept, the place where the items were discovered.' Mr Druze took out his spectacles and polished the lens with a handkerchief. 'No one saw you in Oxford Street, Mr Dibble, at the time of the murder. That is not a question but a fact.' His voice was sharp as if he was addressing a meeting.

'I'm sure plenty of people did, but I don't know who they were,' Archie said.

'It is therefore inconvenient that none has come forward. Perhaps you weren't there at all.'

'I tell you, I was—'

'When did you buy the items for your sisters?'

'The day after Mrs Grady paid me.'

'A whole twenty-four hours later?'

'I had to be sure of their sizes.'

'You did not know their sizes? The sisters you have bought items for before? You did not know their sizes?'

'I wanted them to fit properly—'

'So, you took along one of their dresses and shoes?'

'Yes, yes, that's what I did.'

'A little obvious, wouldn't you say?'

'Obvious?'

'The shop girl remembered you, *obviously*, because of the clothes you brought to show her.'

'What do you mean?' Archie asked, puzzled.

'On the day of the murder, you cannot account for your time from leaving Mrs Grady's house to arriving home.'

'I didn't talk to anyone. I walked slowly; I was just looking in the windows to see what was what. I wasn't in any hurry.'

'Mr Dibble, I put it to you, you were never in Oxford Street that day, but in Knightsbridge murdering Mr Zielinski.'

'No, sir—'

'Yes, sir. Being in Oxford Street is a pack of lies. It is an elaborate ruse—'

'What?'

'Having murdered Mr Zielinski, you needed to establish an alibi—'

'No, no, wait—'

'So, you said you were wandering Oxford Street, intending to buy clothes for your sisters—'

'I was in Oxford Street—'

'To back up your lie, you went to a clothing store the next day, knowing the shop girl would remember such an event—'

'No, I was there on both day—'

'One ruse after the other—'

'Oi! What sort of brief are you?' Mary shouted. 'You're here to get him free not to agree with everything the coppers says.'

Mary was beside herself and gripped the table tightly. Mr Druze, leant back in his chair. His expression was grim.

'This is the case against you, Mr Dibble,' Mr Druze said calmly. He wore a peculiar smile as he spoke. 'For reasons yet to be established, you needed money. You contrived a robbery, stealing cash from your grandfather's till and your grandmother's ring. The ring you pawned in Mr Zielinski's shop. Perhaps later you returned, carrying a knife with you, one of your grandmother's, possibly for protection. A dispute occurred, perhaps one concerning the value of the object pawned, and you murdered Mr Zielinski. Whereupon you ransacked his shop for valuables, took them back to your home and hid them under the floor boards. In the process you lost a glove. The matching right hand pair was found in your room. With your new found wealth, you purchased a not inexpensive dress and a similarly expensive pair of shoes for your sisters. When asked about your whereabouts at the time of the murder you cannot provide an alibi. When visited by Miss Finch, you insisted she slept on a couch in the living room, rather than her usual sleeping place, a bed in the storeroom. No doubt she was directed to sleep elsewhere for fear of discovery of your ill-gotten gains. So, then, that is the police's contention. What say you, sir?'

Archie gazed at him in disbelief, before he dropped his head to hide his face in his hands.

'Wait!' Mary said. 'What about the knife. Archie's not that stupid. Why not wash it and return it to the kitchen? Then no one would know it was missing.'

Mr Druze's smile was shallow. 'Only that he did not. The prima facie case is damning, Miss Finch. We must strive to prove it is incorrect. That will not be easy.'

'What will happen if you don't?' Archie asked.

'In the worst case, you will be sent to the gallows. In the best case, you will be exonerated and freed. The middle ground is more than likely. You will be incarcerated for a considerable time. If the Crown cannot prove murder, they will seek the next best thing.'

'You can't let that happen, Mr Druze,' Mary said.

'Sir Mortimer Willard will lead, and I shall assist,' Mr Druze said.

'Who is he?' Mary asked.

'He shall advocate for us. He will certainly tear the majority of this evidence apart. But even he cannot perform miracles.'

'Mrs Grady did hire me and pay me, sir,' Archie said pleadingly. 'That's the money I used to buy the stuff. She overpaid. But I told her she did and I wanted to return the difference, but she wouldn't hear of it.'

'Have no fear. The widow will speak in your defence to confirm that, Mr Dibble. The fact of your honesty mitigates in your favour.' He nodded several times.

'Then what else is worrying you?' Mary asked.

'That any further relationship between Mr Dibble and Mr Zielinski should be found. That would suggest you lied to the police. And that will hang you.'

Archie jumped up. 'I tell you, sir, I don't know the man. And I don't ever go to Knightsbridge.'

'The prosecution will contend that you did, at least once.'

Archie slapped his palms down against the desk in frustration. He made to speak and slumped into his chair. He was breathing heavily as he gazed silently downwards.

'You will answer no more questions asked of you by the police. Is that clear, Mr Dibble?' the solicitor said. 'You will refer them to me each time they question you.

They will not like it, but they will respect it. Be obdurate.'

'And you'll get him off?' Mary said.

'We shall engage Sir Mortimer Willard forthwith,' he said.

When they left the police station, Mary made her way back to Baker Street. She felt she should stay with the Dibbles and help as best as she could before Monday when she would have to go to work again.

The fog she walked through suited her mood. For the whole week it lingered, neither thinning nor thickening. In the still air, it hung unmoving. She felt things were hidden from her: whatever it was that troubled Mrs Grady, Archie's terrible predicament, and now she remembered last night's attack as she passed the shop where it occurred. So much was happening so quickly, and all at the same time. She did not know which to concentrate on first.

14

CAROLS IN TRAFALGAR SQUARE

WHEN SHE RETURNED to the Dibbles, she helped grandma open the pie shop for business. If she believed it would take the old lady's mind off Archie's predicament, she was sorely mistaken. At times she caught the old lady staring listlessly at nothing in particular, lost in thoughts about her grandson. She was grateful the shop wasn't busy that Saturday. The girls, for the most part, stayed in their room. They were sullen and lifeless, and their unusual silence was strange and disquieting. Later, Dr Watson dropped by to say he had sent a telegram to Mr Holmes.

'I am afraid it will chase him and it may well be several days, if not a week, before he receives it,' he said. 'Even then, Mary, he may not be able to disengage himself easily. However, you can comfort yourself—nothing much will happen until the police conclude their investigations, by which time, I am sure he will be back.'

Mary's head drooped. She knew this only too well, since Mr Holmes told her, that the first few days of investigating a crime were the most crucial. Afterwards, any further investigation would yield diminishing results.

Sunday dawned cold and foggy. Archie's arrest by now had made the newspapers. Even though it was just a small item, Mary read it glumly before hiding it, not wishing any of the Dibbles to see it and get upset.

ARREST MADE IN KNIGHTSBRIDGE PAWNBROKER'S MURDER CASE.

Police have arrested a 16-year-old-boy in connection with the murder of Janusz Zielinski in Knightsbridge. Inspector Baynes, who is investigating the case, said: 'We are continuing to appeal for witnesses in relations to the investigation. In particular for anyone who was in and around the Marshall & Snelgrove department store between the hours...'

BELOW THE STORY WERE TWO SMALLER NEWS ITEM: *THE case of the Earl of Marshmere versus Mr James Grimwig will be heard on Friday...* And, a man was found badly beaten in an alley off Oxford Street last Friday. *Police were seeking information.*

On several occasions, she and grandpa tried to visit Archie at the Bow Street police station, only to be turned away—he was still being questioned. Mr Druze had been present, but he made no comments when he saw them.

By early Sunday afternoon, Mrs Grady's ward, Ella Sutton, along with the maids, Fortune Dubois and Kitty, arrived at the pie shop. Usually, Sossie and Dot would be happy to see them, and an explosion of noise would follow. But today, they all quietly got ready and trudged morosely towards Trafalgar Square, where the Salvation Army had a choir. With Christmas not two weeks away, Mary shared Grandma's hopes that the carols would cheer them up. Listening to the choir was something she'd done annually since she first arrived at the Dibbles, that year she ran away from Mrs Fortesque.

They met up with Emma Watkins, a maid Mary worked with when they were both employed by the Grimwigs. She now worked for the Earl of Marshmere. The position of Lady's maid was given to her on the recommendation of Sherlock Holmes. Emma brought along Sydney Bottle, a thin man, with a ruddy complexion. He stood a good foot and some taller than Emma. He was an up-and-coming journalist with the Telegraph newspaper, and was her husband-to-be.

'So, how's it all going?' Emma asked. 'This new job? They keeping you busy?'

Mary frowned, she screwed up her nose, then snorted. Closing her eyes tightly, her brows furrowed in concentration, she said: 'Dit dah… Dit dah dah dit. Dit dah. Dit dit. Dah dit… Dit dit. Dah dit… Dah. Dit dit dit dit. Dit…!' She said the last 'dit' particularly loudly, then snorted again.

''Ere, you taken leave of your senses?' Emma said. Around her, the children were giggling.

'No! That's what I'm doing—dit dah-ing all day!'

'Dit what. 'Ere, Syd—' Emma turned only to see Syd laughing.

'Mary's just practising her Morse, Ems,' he said.

'Her what?'

'Her Morse code. So, Mary, you're going to be a telegraphist?'

'Something like that,' Mary said, not willing to say more. Being a woman employed outside of the normal opportunities available to them, domestic servants mainly, was unusual enough. But to be engaged with an organisation she couldn't speak about, would be difficult to explain, even if she were allowed to do so. She quickly changed the subject.

'I met him; did I tell you? Grimwig. On Tuesday,' Mary said.

Emma's mouth fell open. 'So, he's back in London, is he?'

'He ain't changed a bit. Nor have the triplets. Smarmy as ever.'

'What did he say?'

'He still thinks me and Milverton was working

together. He ain't about to forgive me, that's for sure. He still blames me for all that's happened to him.'

'Cheeky so and so.' Emma clucked rudely. ''Ere, the Earl is suing him, don't you know? It's the gossip of the house. Syd's covering the case.'

'My big chance,' Syd said. 'Reporting on court cases is dry stuff, but a few months of it and then I'll be given something meatier.' He beamed happily.

'Look, Mary,' Emma said. 'It's one of Sydney's articles.' She showed her the latest edition of the Telegraph and a report on the findings of an inquest.

It was Charles Augustus Milverton's inquest, as reported by Mr Sydney Bottle. Seeing the blackmailer's name again, she felt his ghost standing beside her and she shivered. Even after all these months, her dealings with the man were all too clear in her mind.

'Emma was telling me about Grimwig,' Syd said. 'A blackmailer as well—'

'Less of being a reporter.' Emma nudged him sharply in the stomach. 'This is my best friend you're speaking to.'

Mary laughed, seeing the look on Emma's face and the wide smile on Syd's. They looked such a happy couple. She was glad. Emma truly deserved to be so fortunate and to find someone like Syd.

'Thanks in advance for taking the girls back to Baker Street, Ems,' she said. 'I appreciate that. I really must get back to my rooms tonight.'

'It isn't a problem,' Emma said. 'I ain't seen the Dibbles for ages. How's Archie coping?'

Mary shrugged. 'As well as can be expected under the circumstances.' She didn't want to speak more, there was far too much to explain.

'You get off home, afterwards,' Syd said. 'We'll drop the others at Mrs Grady, as well. Here, Ems, I wonder if she'll agree to be interviewed about the Grey Lady affair?'

'Sydney!' Emma said. 'Stop being a reporter.'

He tapped his nose. 'A good snoop needs to be ready when an opportunity presents itself.'

'Sydney Bottle, I'll thump you, if you *snoop* like that when we're there,' Emma threatened.

'Blimey,' Mary said. 'You ain't hitched yet and you're already arguing like an old married couple.'

'No, we're not, because he knows who wears the trousers,' Emma said and she lifted her head proudly, much to Syd's delight and amusement.

'Come on, let's talk about happier stuff and enjoy ourselves.' Mary nodded to the choir, who were standing resplendent in their uniforms amongst the crowd that was gathering.

'Cor, I love a sing-song,' Emma Watkins said. She leant over to give Mary a firm hug.

'You've got a good 'un, here,' Mary said to Syd. 'And don't you ever forget it.' She waggled a finger at him.

'You don't need to tell me,' he said with delight. He tipped his hat at a rakish angle and reached a long arm around Emma's shoulder, drawing her near.

'Blimey, you'll be Mr and Mrs Sydney Bottle this time next year,' Mary said.

'Mrs Bottle!' Emma giggled and blushed. In the cold night air, her cheeks, already red, positively glowed.

As if on cue, the choir struck up *'O Come, All Ye Faithful'*, their voices filling Trafalgar Square with delicious harmonies. A clock chimed the evening hour. The air greyed and the London Particular was thickening. Thin as the fog was, it was building its presence by the minute and promised to be a peasouper before long. Just then, a light dusting of snow began falling, swirling around the people and around the lanterns some carried, seemingly dancing merrily to the tune. A cheerful captain of the Salvation Army, wandering amongst the crowd, rattled his collection box next to Mary. She quickly dug inside her purse, taking out tuppence and deposited it into his tin. Her friends did the same. Then they all joined in with the chorus, singing heartily, if sometimes out of tune.

Eventually, when the last carol was sung, there was a disappointing sigh from the crowd, followed by enthusiastic clapping and bravo-ing. As the crowd dispersed, the friends wandered towards one of the fountains. On a bitterly cold December night, the water inside was frozen solid.

Mary said her goodbyes and she left them. She thought how happy Emma and Syd were, and how joyful their meeting was. Grandma was right, seeing her friends and listening to the carols was just the tonic she needed. Yet as she walked towards home, her mood deepened and the veneer of the evening fell away. For once, she didn't know what to do.

Mr Druze worried that some connection would be discovered between Archie and the murdered man, and now she too worried. Whoever set Archie up, some enemy of his, had been careful and planned this well. She feared he would have prepared for this eventuality. Whoever it was had a stroke of luck: at the time of the murder, Archie had no alibi, he was walking aimlessly along Oxford Street, peering into shops but not going in.

She shook her head. Just who would want him hanged? Archie had no enemies. At least none that would go to these lengths. The whole affair spoke of utter hatred. She, on the other hand, was different. She had those sorts of enemies, such as Mr Grimwig and his evil butler, Mr Boots. And the death of Milverton was the catalyst that brought her old employer back into her life. With that thought, she became aware of the slow tapping of footsteps from somewhere behind her. A shiver, like iced water running down her back, made her tremble.

Mary glanced around. The fog was thick. The nearer the river she went, the denser it became. Now it was diffi-cult to make out those around her; the fog turned them into shadows. She hurried along Whitehall, suddenly fearful, remembering what happened recently. It was no accident that caused her to fall down the steps of the shop in Oxford Street, she'd been deliberately pushed. Briefly she contemplated dropping into Deacon House. George Bradley would be on duty; he never went home, they said.

Instead, she hurried away faster only to notice the footsteps were keeping pace with her. She turned off Whitehall and hastened across Westminster Bridge. The clatter of footsteps was gaining, getting closer, following, growing louder.

Now she was running. She went as fast as she could, mindful that she could see nothing ahead of her. Her heart was thumping, her breathing came in quick, sharp gasps. She was halfway across Westminster Bridge when Mary suddenly stopped and turned swiftly. The footsteps stopped just as abruptly. Big Ben rang out the quarter, the chimes muffled in the fuggy air.

'Who's there?' she shouted.

Her eyes jerked sideways.

She strained her ears.

Not a sound other than the slow grinding of carriage wheels, the wheezing of horses and their snorting breaths.

'Come on, show yourself. I know someone's there.'

She listened intently.

Nothing.

Fearful of the dreadful silence, she began to back

away whilst holding her breath. Now all she could hear was her pounding heart, blood swooshing in her ears, her chattering teeth. Despite the cold, she was hot, her face and neck damp with perspiration. She'd just heaved a sigh of relief, the old man she'd bumped into vanished into the gloom when she heard it. Her heart froze. From inside the dense, foul-smelling mustard curtain, from behind her, the clip-clopping of footsteps rushed closer.

❦ II ❧

❧ 15 ❧

A SUICIDE

'*HELP!*' Mary screamed.

'Let's see if you can swim, little darling.' The dark figure laughed. A scarf was drawn across his face, and only his eyes, cold and hard as the night, were visible.

She clutched her attacker tightly, fearful of letting go. He wrenched her hand away and pressed his weight against her. He was slowly pushing her further and further over the railings, over the edge of the bridge. In desperation, Mary grabbed hold of the rails. She heard the swirling waters of the river below her, and all her fears about the Thames returned. Twice she had been in the river, and both times she almost drowned.

'Please, mister, please don't do this,' Mary pleaded.

Then, to her utter surprise, he let her go.

Mary fell sprawling onto the pavement. She was confused. She didn't wait to understand his actions, but quickly scrambled away on all fours from the edge of the bridge towards the safety of the road.

'Where you going?' the man grunted and laughed again.

He grabbed her ankle, dragging her backwards towards the railings once more. Immediately, the realisation of what he was doing washed through her. He was playing with her, teasing her, like a cat batting a mouse around for the pleasure of it before finally pouncing and finishing the job. This was sport. She turned on her back and struck out with her free leg. The man tumbled away. In a tripping stumble, Mary gained her feet as the man lurched towards her again.

'You ain't going nowhere,' he yelled. Grasping her arm, he laughed wildly.

'What the hell did I say?' a grating voice boomed out of the fog from somewhere behind them.

The man's manic laughter stopped, to be replaced by a frightened gasp. Mary watched in fascination as his eyes bulged. His head slewed sharply around. At that moment, his scarf fell away to reveal the fear in his gaping mouth. He released her. In a wild panic, he turned to run just as a figure, a veritable giant, loomed out of the fog and grabbed him.

Her tormentor was being lifted off the ground with consummate ease. He clung to Mary's arms in desperation, dragging her along with him, until she too was being lifted off the ground. Mary clawed at him, twisted and kicked until he released his grip. As she tumbled to the ground, both figures fell back and were lost in the murky gloom.

'You were told the word,' the grating voice growled. 'She's mine, not yours.'

'No. No. Wait!' the man shrieked. 'I didn't mean— What? No! No! Don't! Don't.' Suddenly, he yelled, 'Doooooon't!'

There was a moment of silence. Then a dull splash. Then silence. Mary held her breath. Her heart started crashing great hammering blows. The blood whooshed through her ears. From deep within the mist below her, desperate muffled shouts of help and splashing from someone in the river, reached her.

Mary crept backwards as noiselessly and stealthily as she could. Crouching low, making herself as small as possible, she peered blindly into the curtain of fog, her eyes flicking left and right. The world was deathly quiet. It was as if all the carriages, all the horses, all the drivers on Westminster Bridge were suddenly silenced.

Slowly voices started to come out of the mist.

'Miss, where are you?'

'What's the trouble?'

'Say something so's we can find you.'

Mary tried to shout, but her words caught in her dry throat.

'Where is she, Fred?'

'Has someone fallen in?'

'Was it her?'

'Miss, say something.'

Someone was coming out of the fog. Someone large was emerging, walking slowly towards her. The hairs on her arms prickled. She backed away, hesitantly, until she was leaning once more against the railings. As soon as she touched the cold metal, she saw him: Absalon Furie, the giant. His scarred and tattooed face looked grimly determined. His eyes fixed her.

'There you are,' he growled.

Mary spun away. She ducked past him and tore blindly into the fog in a feral panic. Behind her came the sounds of a fight.

'Oi! Who the hell are you?'

'Watch out, Fred.'

'Here, you get away from me.'

Mary dashed across Westminster Bridge oblivious to any danger. She was less afraid of bumping into anyone, and more of the clattering footsteps and the fight she could hear behind her. On several occasions she almost tripped, skidded on the cobbles or nearly collided with a person or a lamp-post. Somehow, she managed to stay on her feet.

Soon all she could hear was her own footsteps, but regardless, she kept running. Five minutes later, her lungs burning, her breath rasping, and barely able to run further, she found her lodgings.

Mary fiddled the key into the lock, almost dropping it

in her panic. Once inside, she slammed the door shut, drew the several bolts closed, and flew up the stairs, not caring about the racket she made. She found her room, opened it and blazed through the door, slamming and locking it behind her. She jammed a chair under the door handle and then rushed to the kitchen. She found the largest kitchen knife she possessed. Dashing back, pushing the bed away from the wall, she crouched behind it. Almost hiding, she brandished the blade in front of her.

Mary gulped her breath. She was sweating profusely. Her hand holding the knife shook and she could barely keep it still. All she could think about was that Mr Grimwig placed a bounty on her head. She was only saved because the bare-knuckle fighter wanted the reward, instead. And having dealt with her assailant, Furie would have had it, had she not run as if the hounds of hell were on her heels.

Holding her breath, trying to quiet her pounding heart, Mary listened intently to the house that was as quiet as a sleeping church. Imaginary or otherwise, any noise seemed magnified. It would be a long, frightening night, but she was determined to stay awake. She needed to be alert in case Furie turned up. Mary feared he knew where she lived. Minutes seemed to turn into hours and when the adrenalin fuelling her blood dissipated, she slept where she crouched, still in her clothes, only to wake with a start, pulled out of sleep by a dream that *Fire-Fists* Furie was breaking through her door.

To her surprise, the room was flooded with light. The curtains hadn't been drawn. She slept not only the whole evening, but the entire night as well. She was still holding the knife, and her hand ached from clutching it so tightly. Her stiff joints cracked when she stood up from the cold and being confined in one position for so long. She peered out of the window surprised that the sky was a sparkling blue. Flags were fluttering wildly, and the windows rattled like Morse code messages each time the breeze pressed against them. The London Particular was blown away in the night, and the air was clear. A fresh, welcoming wind was blowing in from the east.

Mary pressed her ear up against the door. Not a sound. Gingerly, as silent as she could, she removed the chair from under the doorknob, and turned the key. She opened the door a crack. Keeping her shoulders against it, she peeked out. The corridor was empty. She peered down the stairwell. Nothing. Creeping downstairs, the knife always ahead of her, Mary exhaled the breath she was holding, relieved to find that the bolts were still drawn closed on the front door.

Quickly, she returned to her room, bathed, changed clothes, ate breakfast, and slipped downstairs. Still fearful, she exited the house on guard. Mary scanned the street, up and down, several people were walking along, but no one looked out of place, and she couldn't see the giant.

Nonetheless, taking no chances, Mary dashed to Westminster Bridge. Once there, she felt safer in and amongst the others using it that morning, but not so safe as to prevent her from looking around and behind, several times as she crossed it.

There was a gathering at Westminster Pier. She spied several policemen standing in a huddle. The man, the one who attacked her, the one thrown into the river, was that why they were there? She rushed along remembering it could have been her instead of him. Once she reached the front door of Deacon House, she knocked heavily. Tommy Tiggs let her in. The first thing she saw was the concern on George Bradley's face.

'Tiggs told me what happened Friday,' he said. 'But that look says something else happened. Let's have it?' he demanded.

Mary quickly explained her confrontation in the fog and the policemen on the pier. She made no mention of Archie's arrest.

Mr Bradley rose from behind his desk. 'Mind the store, Tiggs,' he said. 'And you, Mary, go and see the major and tell him what's occurred.' With that, he left.

She found the major occupied the same way he was that day she signed the document. This time, he placed his umbrella down, ordered tea, and sat with her.

Mary related her story. She told him she worked for

the Grimwigs, how she was accused of theft and how she survived her encounter with Black Bob. She told him about Milverton's part and the blackmail of the Earl of Marshmere by Mr Grimwig. She spoke about Grimwig's butler, Mr Boots, someone they both knew, who was now languishing behind bars.

'You suspect Grimwig is out for revenge?' The major pondered. He gazed at the window as if searching there for his answer, even though the question was a rhetorical one.

Nevertheless, Mary answered. 'He's hired this man, Furie, and it was him that chased me.'

The major's eyes rose at the mention of the name. There was a knock on the door.

'Come!' he shouted and George Bradley entered.

'Been down to Westminster Pier, sir,' he said. 'A small-time leg-breaker named Simmonds tried to commit suicide last night.'

'Tried?'

'He jumped off the bridge.'

The major smoothed back his moustache. A small smile curled the edges of his mouth.

'He probably thought he stood a better chance in the Thames,' he said, 'than against Furie. A wise decision. This Simmonds…?'

'He's thawing out at St Barts, sir. I don't reckon he'll have much to say for himself.'

The major rose and went to perch his weight on the window sill.

'Well, we can't give Mary twenty-four-hour protection, and there is little point in telling the police—the lack of proof is evident. They would maintain it was hearsay and it would draw too much attention to ourselves. And this Simmonds won't compromise himself.'

'Tiggs could keep an eye on Mary, sir.'

'Tiggs? Against Furie? A little mismatched in weight, wouldn't you say?'

Mr Bradley, suppressing a grin, said, 'I mean, keep an eye out, sir. Four eyes are better than two.'

'Yes. I see what you mean.' The major went and stood with his back to the fire, warming his hands. 'At least we shall have a reliable witness to Mary's murder,' he joked.

Mary huffed inwardly. This wasn't a joke as far as she was concerned.

'Yes. Tiggs will escort you home and to work for the next few days, Mary. Keep to the open road, no excursions into dark alleys. Lock all the doors and make sure you know who is knocking before you open them.'

'Furie, sir?' Mr Bradley asked.

'Get the dogs and find him and his friend. We cannot have some so-and-so threaten our promising apprentice, can we? She's family, after all.'

Mary left the major's office; he was still talking to

Bradley. She found Tommy and told him of the major's request. His face immediately brightened.

'Blimey, Miss,' he gushed. 'You're a right one, for sure. My stars! Jupiter! It's my chance!' He punched the air.

She wondered if Tommy fully understood. It was not so much that he'd stepped out of the frying pan and into the fire, as having stepped straight into the flames, ignoring the pan completely.

'Well, since you're my escort, I have two tickets for the Theatre Royal. I think it's one of Mr Frobisher's tests. Want to come?'

'*Robinson Crusoe!* Do I?'

With that, she wandered towards the basement, where Frobisher was waiting patiently. He motioned for her to sit in a chair next to his desk. He then removed the dust-cover from the telegraph device and gave Mary an exercise—to tap out a message he'd written. He left for another room, where Mary knew there was the corresponding receiving device. From then until the end of the day, they indulged in Morse code conversations—something she was becoming proficient at.

Concentrating fully on decoding his replies and encoding her messages filled her mind, and thoughts of Furie and Archie's predicaments were soon put aside.

16

A MEETING AT THE THEATRE

AT THE END of the day, Tommy Tiggs escorted her home. He took great pride in the task, and kept a sharp lookout for anything unusual. He puffed himself up like a courting pigeon, and strutting just as importantly, maintained a dour expression with narrowed eyes. His steely determination was evident as he insisted on entering her lodging house first. He checked the staircase, each of the bathrooms on the landings, and went into her room before her, where he took a good look around before allowing her inside. The following day, he was waiting beside her front door to escort her to work.

'I just wished they'd given me a gun,' he complained. 'Just in case…'

'Have you ever fired one?' Mary asked.

'Well, not exactly. Granddad has an old revolver and

he showed me how to use it.' With that, he patted the bag slung over his shoulder.

'What's in there?' Mary nodded, curious as to the bag's content.

Tommy beamed broadly and opened the cloth bag and Mary startled.

'It's granddad's revolver. It's his old Colt Dragoon,' Tommy said. He stepped inside the doorway for privacy, and took out the gun. Mary's mouth dropped open. The revolver was well over a foot long. The barrel was certainly over seven inches in length. When he handed it to Mary, she almost dropped it. It weighed in excess of four pounds.

'It's bigger than you,' she said.

'A real man-stopped,' Tommy boasted. 'This'll stop Furie, I bet.'

'Stop a bleedin' elephant, I expect.'

Tommy sighed in disappointment. 'Unfortunately, it needs percussion caps, powder and special bullets.'

Mary didn't know much about firearms, but enough to know that this one didn't take the usual type of ammunition, and each of the six chambers had to be loaded in an old-fashioned way.

'Is there a point having it, then?' she asked.

'It's just for show.' Tommy's face brightened. 'It's all about what Mr Bradley says. You got to show them you mean business.'

Mary doubted that Tommy quite understood Mr

Bradley, just as she was sure that *they* would not be very impressed with a gun that didn't work.

'Well, you could always beat them to death with it,' she said. 'It weighs enough.'

'I reckon it'll put them off their stride long enough for us to leg it,' he said.

Mary admitted, it was a plan of sorts. She just hoped, for more reasons than she'd care to say, that they would never have to use it.

They strolled across Westminster Bridge. Mary checked her watch against the time on Big Ben. Satisfied, she continued walking. The day was bright and fresh. The air smelled clean compared to the last several days, which had been fetid and pungent. With a cloudless sky, it was bitterly cold.

'You forgetting we're going to the theatre tonight?' Mary said.

Tommy grunted, no, he hadn't. He was wearing his best clothes.

'You going to carry that there?' She indicated the bag with the gun.

'Uh! Huh.'

'Seriously?'

'Yes. Why?'

She shook her head and smiled. She warmed to Tommy.

By some miracle, Tommy managed to slip the gun

past Mr Bradley who wasn't his usual eagle-eyed self that morning.

At the end of the day, she rushed along to Baker Street with Tommy in tow. Grandma made a pie for Archie. She was dubious that he was being fed properly. After a quick meal, they went to Bow Street.

'You better hide that,' Mary said to Tommy, pointing to the bag. 'The coppers won't be too pleased if they find that monster. And wait for me outside, otherwise they'll search you.'

Before meeting with Archie, the policeman, the same one who rummaged through the bag of clothes she brought to Archie a few days ago, eyed the pie she carried.

'Is this the one with the file inside?' he asked. He sniffed it. 'Hmmmm! Steak and kidney.' And then licked his lips.

'You ain't getting any,' Mary said haughtily, and the policeman looked playfully hurt.

Archie tucked into the pie greedily, speaking with his mouth full.

He said, Mr Druze returned with a posh gent, Sir Mortimer Willard, only that morning. The gent was slippery as an eel.

'It is up to the crown to prove their case, Mr Dibble, Sir Willard said,' Archie related. 'We must sow doubt in the minds of the jurors. You are innocent until proven guilty.'

Mary wanted to say something, but Archie looked happier than she had seen him look the past few days. From deep inside her, a little devil nagged and refused to be silent; it was Druze's worry that some connection would be found between the dead pawnbroker and Archie. She had few doubts that all that had happened was far too well planned. She couldn't help thinking that some connection would be found. She was all too aware that people had been hanged on less evidence.

She forced such thoughts from her mind. It was too awful to think about. Archie was her best friend. The Dibbles were her family. She prayed that Sherlock Homes had received Dr Watson's telegram and was hurrying back. Despite the praise given to him by Dr Watson, Inspector Baynes was, after all, a policeman, and they had their man as far as they were concerned—solving a crime like murder would be a substantial feather in his cap.

She left the police station despondent. For a second, she contemplated forgetting about the theatre and just going home. But she knew that wouldn't help her humour. With little to do at home but read, she'd worry instead.

It was a short walk to the theatre—down Bow Street, left into Russell Street and there it was. Tommy, following like a faithful guard dog, glared daggers at anyone who came too near Mary. His eyes constantly flicked left and right. His resolve was resolute—he would not go down without a fight—he would discharge his duties faithfully and bravely. Even so, Mary knew, he would not trouble *Fire-Fists* Furie in the slightest. Nevertheless, she was glad of his company. They queued up under the portico amongst the other theatre-goers. When the doors opened, they pushed their way through.

From the dark street, they entered into a blaze of lights and a buzz of conversation that echoed off the walls and filled the foyer with noise. She was excited. Mary always loved the theatre—not the serious theatre, all that Shakespeare stuff and those Greek tragedies—but she enjoyed comedy and pantomime, immensely. The music hall she particularly liked. She was, nevertheless, glad of the present Emma gave her when they met in Trafalgar Square. Reading *Hamlet* would give her a chance to reconsider her bias.

Their seats were in the front row of the upper circle. She peered over the edge. It was a fair drop. Tommy glanced around nervously and insisted he took the aisle seat. Any assassin would have to get through him first.

'What do you think *the Prof* meant when he sent you the tickets?' Tommy asked.

Mary hunched. 'I've no idea.'

She looked around as if trying to spot a clue. There would be some code here, somewhere, or something to do with her employment.

She played through the recent exercises she and *the Prof* had done to see if there was a connection between them and this. Nothing as far as she could tell. They'd bought a programme. She scanned that. Nothing came to mind. The seat and row numbers? No. Maybe the theatre's address? She shook her head. This test was harder than the rest. Maybe it will be something on the stage or something the actors say. As the lights dropped and the audience hushed, she sat back, determined at least to enjoy the evening, if nothing else.

As soon as the theatre descended into darkness, Tommy was alert and tensed. He sat on the edge of his seat, ready at a moment's notice. Halfway through the first act, a man arose from the centre of their row of seats and made his way to the aisle. Tommy was anxious as he approached them. It was a long drop into the stalls below, and he was a big enough man to just pick Mary up and throw her over the edge.

He apologised for disturbing them.

Mary sat back, drew in her legs and allowed him to pass. Tommy's eyes followed him as he walked up the aisle. The boy released the breath he was holding. When he returned, Tommy eyes him suspiciously. However, the man merely apologised once more and made his way along to his seat.

Before long, both she and Tommy were guffawing and bellowing laughter along with the several hundred others in the theatre. A wide smile was permanently spread across their faces.

At the end of the first act, Mary stood up. She

stretched her arms. Still giggling, they wandered down the stairs and outside to get some fresh air.

They stood near the portico, now ablaze with lights and with others similarly getting air, and continued laughing. She was just about to remind Tommy of something they had seen when the smile slipped from her face. From a door at the entrance of the theatre, Mr Grimwig, his wife Dora, and the triplets emerged. He glanced around, puffing deeply on a cigarette, and then their eyes met. For a few moments, Mary and he stared at each other. Her blood ran cold.

'Mary!' He presented a low, mocking bow, a smirk on his face, and walked up to her. 'Well, fancy meeting you here of all places. Dora, girls. Look. It's Mary Finch.'

'Oh, the maid!' Portia said in a superior tone that caused her sisters to snigger.

'Who're they?' Tommy whispered.

'The Grimwigs,' Mary whispered back.

Tommy looked around nervously. His eyes scanned the shadows as if he was expecting to see Furie. His hand immediately dropped inside the bag. He clutched Mary's arm apprehensively and protectively with the other.

17

A SHOT IN THE DARK

MR GRIMWIG POSED an arrogant stance in front of Mary, with his head cocked at an angle, and one hand on his hip. His smirk quickly became a wider, more wicked one.

'Well, what a surprise. Who would have thought we'd meet Mary here, Dora?' he said.

'You don't scare me. I know it's you trying to kill me.' Mary's words came out before she knew she'd spoken them.

'Well, that is uncommonly handsome of you, Miss Finch. You are a caution, I must say.' The smirk on Mr Grimwig's face broadened. 'I have not laid eyes on you for many months and here you are, slandering me, accusing me of murder no less. Kill you? Seems as if you're still alive—much the pity. Or am I addressing Mary Finch's ghost?'

'Is the runt her man?' Dora asked and sniffed at Tommy.

The boy stiffened and scowled at her.

'Now, now Dora, you know as well as I, her man is not available tonight on account of being locked up in a Bow Street cell.'

'Oh, silly me, for not remembering.' She tittered.

'Speaking of murder, you do know, Archie has committed one, don't you, Dora?' Grimwig said and looked mockingly appalled.

'Murder, Jim? Surely not murder?' Dora's hands shot up to her mouth in horror. When she removed them, she wore a oily grin. At that same moment, the triplets, giggled among themselves.

'Gambling debts, I heard, Dora,' Mr Grimwig whispered loudly.

'What are you lot talking about?' Mary asked.

'The boy was a secret gambler?' Dora whispered back, equally loudly so Mary could hear, and looking suitably appalled.

'Apparently.'

'Archie never gambled in his life,' Mary said.

'The things we discover about people, Jim.' Dora continued revelling, ignoring Mary.

'I know, Dora. And he lost heavily, I was told.'

'You mean, he is in debt?'

'Quite a bit.'

'Tut! Tut! And he killed for that!'

'Stole his grandmother's wedding rings and pawned it, I have been told,' Mr Grimwig added loudly.

'Heavens! Girls! You would never do something like that, would you?' Mrs Grimwig clutched at her ring.

'Of course, we would not, mama,' they said in unison, the parody of shock on their faces.

'He'll hang, you do know that, Dora.'

'But only if he's found guilty, Jim.'

'Oooo, the evidence, Dora. The evidence. Damning stuff.'

'Hanging stuff, don't you mean, Jim?' She giggled.

Mary's mouth dropped open in disbelief. Her face burned in anger. They were taking such great pleasure in Archie's discomfort that she stuttered, unable to form her words properly.

'Or else he'll be breaking stones on Dartmoor, I shouldn't wonder.' Dora made a slight movement of her hand to suggest a hammer being wielded, and they both laughed.

'The knife and loot were found under the floorboards of his house, I do believe, Dora?'

'What a stupid place to hide it.'

'How did you know?' Mary barked. 'The papers never reported that?'

Mr Grimwig gazed aimlessly upwards into space and cupped his chin. 'I wonder how I knew that?' he mused.

'And you knew about grandma's ring,' Mary said. 'That weren't reported either.'

'Must be a lucky guess, Jim.'

'Must be, Dora.'

They both cackled.

Mary rubbed the tips of her fingers together, contemplating the two crowing demons, when suddenly her mouth gaped and her eyes widened with the horrible realisation. She caught her breath.

'You!' she shouted. 'You did it!' She stepped forward, flinging Tommy's hand away from her arm. 'You framed him. You did it. It was you!'

'Slander. Slander. We may have to sue, Jim.' Dora laughed.

'What possible reason would we have of setting the boy up? Can you think of one, Dora?'

Dora Grimwig pouted childishly and looked aimlessly upwards before screwing up her nose and shaking her head.

'Not—a—one—Jim.'

'You framed him to get even with me?' Mary said. 'And you tried to murder me?' James Grimwig's expressionless gaze fixed hers. His silence said all she needed to know. 'You hate me that much?' she whispered.

'Enough to see your friend hang,' Grimwig snarled under his breath.

Mary fell quiet, suddenly speechless. She stared at him in utter astonishment. Then suddenly, she came to herself. It was as if someone threw a bucket of cold water over her. She was shaking with rage and she balled her hands into fists. As she looked into his mocking face, she saw the truth clearly. She wanted to punch him and enjoy the great pleasure that would bring her, but she knew it would be pointless—if she was to help Archie, she needed to use her brains, not her fists. Instead, she gritted her teeth and gave a low, unladylike curse before turning completely around to cool her temper. She could feel his smirk behind her back, and she seethed in anger.

At that moment, a frightful scream shattered the air.

'Grimwig!'

Every eye turned towards he who shouted.

Mr Grimwig's head shot up, and the smile vanished completely. He edged backwards, towards the safety of the crowd that gathered under the portico, who were now looking at him. Then, in a frightful panic, as if seeing a ghost, he scuttled away in a tripping stumble across the road.

A dark figure, with a scarf drawn across his face, rushed past Mary and caught him.

'You remember me, Grimwig?' the figure screamed. 'Blackmail me, will you?' he bellowed. 'Think I'm just gonna sit and let a leech like you suck me dry. Think again!'

In an instant, he'd dragged Mr Grimwig completely across the road and bundled him inside the mouth of a dark opening, an archway leading to a courtyard of a large block of flats.

'Help! Help!' Dora Grimwig screamed. She stood rooted to the spot as if paralysed.

Suddenly, there was a flash and a bang from inside the archway. Everyone jumped. Dora Grimwig gasped and yelled, as if in pain. She broke free from whatever force held her and rushed headlong, fearlessly into the dark space where her husband was taken. Her children dashed after her. From inside the archway, her scream, the howl of a wounded beast, shattered the air. At that instance, everyone converged towards her.

Dora rushed out and back into the light and grasped her children. Her face was a mask of terror. Her trembling hands were bloody.

'A doctor!' she bellowed. 'Someone, get a doctor. He's shot my Jim.'

'*Papa!*' the girls shouted and tried to push past their mother. She held them tightly.

Almost immediately there came a shout from the crowd. 'Let me through. I'm a doctor. Damn it, make way.'

The doctor pushed past the crowd and entered the archway. There was a dreadful hush. Mary could just make him out in the darkness, crouched in the shadow, examining the prone figure of Mr Grimwig. She caught a gleam in his eyes as he looked up to where Dora Grimwig and her children stood, four small islands between the crowd and the doorway, illuminated by a streetlamp. The doctor rose slowly, and picking up Mr

Grimwig's cape where it was dropped, he threw it across the body. He exited slowly and stood in front of Dora Grimwig and her children.

'Madam,' he said solemnly. 'I am sad to inform you. Your husband is dead.'

The four Grimwigs screamed, and as Dora collapsed, her daughters caught her.

'Someone, find a policeman,' the doctor said. 'Bow Street police station is nearby. Hurry.'

Mary pushed her way to the back of the crowd. Tommy followed her. She reached the other side of the road, where she stood in silence. She'd gone pale. It'd happened so fast. Despite her observational ability, she could barely recall the man who kidnapped and then shot Mr Grimwig. He was tall, dark, slim. He had a hat drawn across his face and a scarf wrapped around his mouth. He wore ordinary clothes. But beyond that, there was nothing about him that she could point to and say: Yes! That was unique.

For many minutes, the crowd stood silent until a murmur began. It grew and grew as passers-by gathered to see what the commotion was. Soon, the shrill call of police whistles broke through the air. Before long, the constabulary arrived and began the task of clearing the crowd and finding witnesses.

An ambulance from Charing Cross Hospital came.

The doctor was still attending Mrs Grimwig, the girls still crouched beside their mother, when Inspector

Baynes arrived. The policeman looked at the body for a minute before kneeling beside Dora Grimwig. As he did, the doctor immediately stood and went to tend to Dora's children. After a while, the inspector, glancing all around and spying Mary, arose and strolled leisurely across the street towards her. No doubt, Dora Grimwig told him she was there.

'A frightful thing to witness,' he said. 'You knew him, I believe. I spoke to Dr Watson earlier…' he added as an explanation.

'Is-is-is he really dead?' Mary asked.

'A bullet to the head tends to be fatal,' he said. Mary shivered. 'His many debtors are going to be disappointed. Let them try and sue a dead man.'

'Why did someone kill him?' she asked softly.

'Because of Milverton, I'd hazard a guess!' the policeman said matter-of-factly. His sharp eyes gleamed in the lamplight. 'Kill one blackmailer, and the victims gets it in their head to kill another. It was bound to happen.'

'You've caught him… the man… who…?'

'Escaped through the flats. We're looking for witnesses.' He shook his head slowly, as if to say he wasn't hopeful.

'It happened so quickly,' Mary said.

The policeman nodded, as if understanding how unnerved she was.

'Is Mrs Grimwig all right?' Mary asked. Suddenly,

and she didn't know why, given all that happened between her and her husband, she felt sorry for the widow. Despite their history, she didn't wish him murdered.

'As well as can be expected. I can't speak for how she will feel later. I'm afraid she'll have to officially identify the body. A necessary formality that is best done sooner.'

Mary's eyes were fixed on the archway, where two ambulance porters entered. She trembled again.

'Get yourself home, Miss Finch, the air is cold,' Inspector Baynes said, mindful that it was not the air that caused her to shiver. 'I'll speak to you when your mind is more settled. For now, I will have to accompany the widow to the morgue.'

Mary knew she had to tell him.

'Inspector, Mr Grimwig more or less said he was the one that set Archie up.' She looked up pleadingly, then she looked to where Mr Grimwig lay. 'Where does that leave Archie?'

'The same place we were before. It would be your word against his and he is dead.'

'But Tommy heard him say it as well.'

'If his wife was present, she will deny anything of the sort was said.'

'But maybe others overheard—'

'You and Grimwig had a disagreement. He dismissed you. No one likes being dismissed. You understand what

I am saying?' The inspector took a deep breath. Something troubled him; it was written in his face.

'What is it?' Mary asked.

'A witness has come forward—a disreputable character to be sure—who says Archie liked a flutter on the horse. He has proof that Archie owed a substantial sum of money—'

'No!' Mary screamed.

'Calm yourself, Miss Finch.'

'No! Don't you see?' She grabbed the policeman's arm. 'It's what Grimwig planned. He wants revenge on me and he's doing it through Archie.'

Inspector Baynes waved a constable over and pried her hands loose.

'Escort the young lady home… 251,' he said, peering at the number on the constable's collar. 'Take your friend, go home and rest, Miss Finch.' He wore a fatherly expression, and added, 'Whatever you recall, tell 251 on your journey.'

Baynes turned away. Despite Mary's protests, the constable took her elbow. As they left, Mary shuddered. The two porters lifted the body of Mr Grimwig onto a stretcher. Under the sheet that had been thrown on her old employer, the body appeared stiff and awkward, and the porters struggled.

18

TWO TICKET STUBS

THE NIGHT SEEMED ENDLESS. With Grimwig dead, and now a witness who she was sure lied, citing her best friend as a gambler, she wondered if things could get any worse for Archie. This was what Mr Druze feared. Slowly, the case against Archie Dibble was growing and not in his favour. A noose was being tightened around his neck. She paced the room well into the early hours, counting each nail that was being driven into her best friend's coffin.

When morning eventually crept through the blinds, she'd neither slept a wink, nor had she a plan to aid her friend. Still weary, she made her way to work. The news of last night's happenings preceded her. She saw it in George Bradley's demeanour when he said Major Carshaw wanted to see her.

Mary's explanation of recent events was a mere

formality; the major already knew the details. Nevertheless, he listened patiently, smoothing his thin moustache
with a finger, and at the end of her recounting he
walked to the window and gazed out at the street
below.

'An unfortunate incident,' he said. 'You still believe
this Grimwig also tried to kill you?'

'I think so, sir.'

'Well, that part should stop now that he's dead. Hope-
fully the widow will not take up the cause. As for your
friend…' He paused and shook his head and fell quiet. It
was clear from his unspoken comments that he did not
think much of Archie's chances. Instead, he waved her
away. Whether he was satisfied with her account, he did
not say.

On her way to the basement, she passed the reception.
The guilty look Tommy Tiggs wore caused Mr Bradley to
laugh. No doubt he'd already spoken to the major.

'Some secret agent, you!' he said to the boy. 'A poker
face, son, a poker face.' He slapped him on the back and
Tommy shook. 'Don't blame Tiggs, Mary. He had a job
to do and he's done it well.'

Mary smiled at Tommy, who she was glad to have
had as company.

She found Frobisher much the same as when she'd
left him the previous day. He was crouched behind his
small desk, curled in such a fashion, giving the impression of a stick insect in his awkward pose. As usual, he

was fiddling with something. She needed to tell him she'd failed his test.

'Sorry I'm late, Mr Frobisher,' Mary apologised.

He merely nodded. She removed her coat and went to make them a cup of tea.

'I didn't do a good job last night at the theatre,' she said.

'You must keep your wits about you in such situations,' he said without looking up.

'Well, I missed the second half, so if it was there, well, I missed the whole second act.'

'Observation must become second nature.'

'I even bought a programme. But honestly, whatever it was evaded me.' She showed him the programme, but as usual, Frobisher merely nodded without looking up.

'You must recognise when events are unfurling and attune the mind,' he said.

'I even tried to work out if maybe the seat numbers had something to do with it.' She made a face and hunched as if in defeat.

'Focus. Focus. Always focus. A single-minded focus is required.'

'Then maybe, I thought it was something the actors might say.'

'And always review it in your mind immediately afterwards—when it is fresh and unsullied.'

'I even checked their names. But afterwards I thought it must have been in the second act—'

'There are triggers that can be employed. Think about what happened before the event.'

'But as I said, I missed the second act all together—'

'Categorise what occurred. Smells. Colours. A sound you heard. Where did everyone stand? Where did you stand?'

Mary's brow creased as she glanced over to Frobisher. The man's head was still down. He was still concentrating on whatever he was doing while speaking.

'Mr Frobisher… I'm trying to apologise for failing your test.'

'Test? Test? What test?' he said, without raising his head.

'The tickets you sent me… for the theatre…'

'Tickets? What tickets? What are you speaking about?'

'These,' Mary said, finding the ticket stubs in her coat pocket.

He raised his head slowly, a puzzled expression on his face.

'Miss Finch, pray give me an explanation,' he said calmly, if slightly condescendingly. 'I am speaking about the lack of your observational skills at a critical moment. You are speaking about…?'

'The test, sir. The tickets you sent me to go to the theatre and… well… to find out something… like the code you gave me in the envelope… Oh! No! It wasn't somehow written on the tickets, was it?'

The Prof continued to look mystified.

'Miss Finch. I did not send you tickets for the theatre. Do not confuse me with any secret admirers you may have.'

'But, sir,' she gawped and quickly closed her mouth tightly.

'I see we will have to work further on your surveillance skills.' He stared off into space for a moment before patting the seat next to him, saying, 'Come!' a hint of disappointment in his voice. Lifting up a small metal plate that he had been fiddling with, he said, 'This is a combination lock to a safe. This is how they work.'

She barely heard him as he explained the workings of the lock; how each turn of the knob caused various wheels to rotate, pushing the drive pins into place; how the notches on each wheel engaged when the main wheel was spun.

Mary's mind raced. She'd assumed *the Prof* sent her the ticket as one of his tests. That was clearly not the case. If he didn't send her the tickets, then who sent them? She knew of no one who would do such a thing, at least not without a note to explain why.

If Emma Watkins did, it would be with the aim of them going together. Emma would have made that clear. And surely, she would have mentioned it when they met at the carol singing in Trafalgar Square. And yesterday wasn't Emma's night off.

The tickets, though, arrived at the Dibbles. Whoever

sent them must not have known where she now lived, but knew of her association with the pie shop. That ruled out Frobisher, he could easily find her address from the records held at Deacon House.

She had few friends who could afford such a gift and play such a joke. Though what was funny about sending theatre tickets anonymously eluded her.

'Use your ears,' Frobisher continued speaking. 'Listen carefully and you will hear each pin drop into place.'

She complied mechanically. Unable to concentrate, she heard nothing. He nodded, as if affirming the silence. Only when he attached a statoscope did she hear the clicks clearly, but she couldn't discern which from which. With her thoughts elsewhere, she was slow in picking up the lesson. She was brought back to the present when Frobisher huffed loudly.

'It is clear your mind is elsewhere, Miss Finch. I must say, your brother was far more studious!'

'Danny?' Mary startled. 'You knew Danny?'

'Good. I am glad to see I have your attention.' With that, he tapped the metal plate with his pencil. 'Let us begin again.'

'But you couldn't have taught him here… not with all these people about… it would have had to be in a secret place—'

This time, he tapped her head with the pencil. 'Ah!

Some of your skills are still in residence. Good.' Then impatiently, he tapped the metal plate again.

She did not press the matter further, she doubted he'd say more. The major made one thing clear the day she accepted the job: this place *was* all about secrets.

That morning, she was a poor student. The intricacies of a combination lock safe were not foremost in her mind. Frobisher, though, was a hard taskmaster, and wouldn't let her rest. When he was satisfied that she understood the principle, she taken to another room in Deacon House. Several different combination lock safes sat waiting to be opened. Mary spent most of the day trying to break into them and failing miserably each time. To her surprise, Frobisher was pleased with her progress. She wasn't.

'It would be remarkable,' he said, 'had you managed to open one. But you came near!'

The news of the murder made the afternoon editions of the newspaper. She was seated in the canteen drinking tea and eating a sugar bun, and it returned her mind to recent events.

James Grimwig, Business Man, Murdered, the headlines screamed. He'd fallen on hard times, the article said. Money was owed.

Grimwig was a well-known man for the papers to speculate the motive for his murder. Accordingly, it was clear that the culprit could have been an angry debtor, or some failed business partner, or some old enemy. A man in his position would acquire them like moths around a candle. Or it could have been a random incident, a mad man intent on butchery. However, the papers didn't yet know of Grimwig's other business.

But Mary knew. The man screamed blackmail, and Inspector Baynes more or less confirmed that.

The report suggested the widow had completed the dreadful task of identifying the body. She'd broken down at the morgue soon after, and had to be assisted back to her home. She'd already fainted once when the doctor informed her that her husband was dead, so was it any surprise she should faint again, seeing his dead body? A gloomy paragraph sympathised with the children. To have witnessed such an act was truly dreadful, a tragedy, indeed. A further paragraph was a quote from Inspector Baynes, requesting anyone with information to contact him at Scotland Yard. A small reward was offered by the widow. An inquest was arranged for the next week.

Tommy came to sit beside her.

'I don't get it. These tickets,' she said, holding out the stubs toward him. 'Who sent them?' Her fingers drummed on the table, a habit she had when thinking.

The dreadful thought that it was Mr Grimwig came to mind. If so, their meeting was no chance. He'd wanted her there. Was it because he wanted to boast of his cleverness? Evincing some sadistic pleasure to let her know what he'd done and how little she could do about it? How the pair gloated.

A truth dawned on her as she sat there.

Her attacker on Westminster Bridge, wasn't out to murder her. That would never have done. No, it was merely to heap fear on top of fear. Only when Archie was convicted, and she, knowing it was because of her, and could do little to prevent his death, then and only then, would she be murdered. Furie saved her, concerned perhaps that the first attacker had forgotten the plan and threatened to go too far, and for no other reason.

It was clear to her. Grimwig wanted her dead, but not before letting her know his part in Archie's death. He wanted to taunt her. Look at what I've done, and there's nothing you can do about it. She shivered, realising the extent he'd gone to exact his revenge on her. But with Grimwig dead, she wondered, as the major hinted, if the widow would take up the task?

❦ 19 ❦

THE INQUEST

By the end of the week and over the weekend, Mary visited Archie several times. Druze accompanied her on one occasion. He informed Archie that Sir Mortimer Willard was now fully engaged in his case in mind and body. Druze's enthusiasm worried Mary. She had the impression that it was all a show to keep up Archie's spirit. The reason was obvious. This new piece of evidence, this witness who miracled himself into existence, this gentleman who could swear that Archie was a gambler and owed money, clearly worried the solicitor.

To make matters worse, Archie was due to be transferred to a nearby prison. Bow Street cells were needed for local offenders, and on a charge of wilful murder, bail wasn't an option. As she left that day, she could imagine Mr Grimwig, were he alive, laughing and gloating, enjoying his revenge on her through Archie.

Work was a welcome diversion on Monday. She'd fretted the weekend away, her mind clouded with dark, musty thoughts. She threw herself into her tasks. Before the day was out, Mary managed to open several safes, and Frobisher announced that she was on the way to becoming a most admirable *crackswoman*. She welcomed his praise, since he gave them grudgingly—though it wasn't something she could boast about in polite company. When she mentioned this to Tommy, the boy's face flared with excitement. He hinted, excitedly, that there was more than one way to open a safe, and those *other* ways would probably be next. He looked envious.

On Tuesday, the major gave her and Tommy a dispensation to attend the inquest into Grimwig's death. They were to be witnesses. He made it clear, however, that they were attending as private citizens. There was to be no mention of their employer.

The coroner's court on this occasion was in Southwark, only several miles from Mary's lodging house. She walked there and met up with Tommy. The court was housed in an ornate, red-bricked building, surrounded by less than salubrious establishments. But inside, it was all polished wood and marble.

The affair was sombre.

She gave her statement mindful of what the inspector said. She didn't mention the content of her conversation with Grimwig for the fear that it would be taken as unfounded rumours, and told by a former maid with a grudge. She merely stated that their discussion cantered around her employment with him at one time.

Tommy Tiggs could add no more. He, too, had been advised to say as little as possible.

The widow, dressed in black weeds complete with a black veil, dabbed her eyes with a black lace handkerchief throughout her testimony. Nothing was asked of the triplets, and Portia, Rosamund and Leticia sat quietly, dressed appropriately like their mother. For whatever reason, Mary couldn't decide, she felt sorry for them. They could be harpies, but now they were fatherless harpies.

Inspector Baynes was the last in a long line to give evidence. He merely reported the facts as he saw them that day. Grimwig's assailant's description was vague and could fit any number of people. His escape through the flats went unseen.

'And the doctor who attended Mr Grimwig, Inspector, what became of him?' the coroner asked.

The inspector coloured up a tinge of red, and he gave a slight cough into his closed fist.

'We don't rightly know, sir,' he mumbled.

'*You don't rightly know?* What sort of answer is that, Inspector?'

'It appears that in the confusion no one saw fit to take his name and address, sir.'

'Indeed! And how many policemen were there?' The

coroner spied the inspector from under his brow. 'You need not answer that question, Inspector. More than sufficient, I suspect,' he added tartly.

'We have been trying to trace him, but—'

'But, to no avail.' The coroner was clearly unimpressed.

'Being a doctor, sir,' Baynes continued with a smile, 'we assumed he would have known, and have read the notice about the inquest, and would have made himself available.'

'But he hasn't?'

'No, sir.'

'Indeed, sir.'

'However, his evidence is probably… superfluous—'

'You are a doctor?'

'No, sir.'

'When you are, you may speak about things that are unnecessary in that profession.'

Inspector Baynes's small eyes glittered in mirth at his obvious mistake, and he smiled politely and nodded. 'Forgive me, sir. Of course, sir.'

'Thank you, Inspector Baynes. You will attempt to contact the gentleman in question and remind him of his public duty.'

With his affirmation, the inspector removed himself from the witness box. The inquest was over and as the coroner pondered his decision, a small wiry man with bushy black eyebrows, Baynes's junior officer, the very same one who'd found the stolen items at the Dibbles, whispered in the inspector's ear. Baynes immediately left the room.

The coroner's decision came quickly and with little surprise, and his pronouncement was less so: Death by Person or Person's Unknown.

Before the inquest could be dismissed, a dark, brooding, blue-veined-nosed fellow rose from his seat beside the widow. His voice pure gravel, he said, 'Your honour, Poulter. Solicitor to the Grimwigs. The widow… would like the body of her husband… released for cremation… *if* there are no… objections,' he said haltingly.

'Cremation, Mr Poulter?' the coroner asked.

'It was Mr Grimwig's… sincere wishes, sir… to be dealt with, so. He indicated… that to spare his good wife and children… undue worry in the future, it should be done… as soon as possible… upon his demise… so they may carry on with their lives… immediately.'

The coroner looked around, courting any objections. He slowly got to his feet, having received no response.

'I see no reason to not release the body,' he said in an absent-minded way. The proceedings were over and he looked anxious to leave. 'Since there are no doubts concerning the cause of death, the police can have no possible objections, I am sure.'

'Thank you… sir,' the gentleman said, and he resumed his seat beside the widow.

As everyone left the coroner's court, Mary

approached Mrs Grimwig. She'd not forgotten her crowing at the Theatre Royal. But with Archie in jail and soon to be on trial for his life, she felt she had to say something and find some way to help him.

'I know we had our problems, ma'am,' she said. She fidgeted nervously and was glad she couldn't see Mrs Grimwig's eyes clearly behind the black veil. Even so, she clearly felt her glare. 'I am truly sorry for what happened.'

The widow stiffened and straightened her gait. She was holding her breath, keeping her emotions in check.

'I never did thank you for employing me when you did,' Mary continued. 'I was very happy in the Regent's Park house… up until… well, you know… that incident.'

'When you stole from us? When you bit the hand that fed you?' Mrs Grimwig said. She lifted her head high and arrogantly.

'Honestly, ma'am, I know you don't believe me, but I never stole a thing from you. It was just you all thought I did.' Mary fell quiet. It was no use explaining it again. The triplets made a show of turning their backs to her. 'But ma'am,' Mary pleaded, 'it's over, ain't it? Don't take it out on Archie. He ain't done anything to you.'

'My husband is dead, and all that has happened to us was because of *you,*' Mrs Grimwig spat the words at her. 'I hope the boy rots in hell.'

'But Archie's innocent—'

Dora Grimwig swung on her heels and stomped off, her children following.

Mary ground her teeth. She knew it was futile, but she had to try. The irony was not lost on her—having made the lives of many miserable with their blackmail, the Grimwigs were complaining when theirs had being made the same by Milverton, and blaming her.

It promised to be a slow walk back to her lodgings, and Tommy, who decided to keep her company, wanted to take an omnibus. But Mary needed to think, and she often did her best thinking while walking and daydreaming. However, today, her mind was focused on something that didn't make sense, and any daydreaming would have to wait.

Tommy was the cause of her thinking so much, telling her what he'd overheard.

Before leaving, she'd been speaking to Inspector Baynes, who looked particularly morose. The coroner's decision to release the body for the funeral upset him. He'd been out of the room when it was agreed. His annoyance was with his junior, who didn't see fit to object, and whom he couldn't locate. It clearly irked him.

Mary questioned Baynes, trying to find out the name of the helpful citizen who had decided, *no doubt,* from the goodness of his own heart, to share Archie's *gambling habits* with the police. She wanted to know, as well, where the Grimwigs resided. She'd not yet given up hope that she could persuade the widow to leave

Archie alone. It was a desperate desire, but what choice had she?

Inspector Baynes wouldn't part with any information. There was, however, something dark in his mood, something that troubled him that he wouldn't explain. What it was she didn't know, only that she thought it had something to do with Archie. There was something he wasn't telling her.

Baynes, though, didn't tarry, but left, saying he had several arrangements to make before the body would be released. He took time, though, to advise her to leave the investigation to him. When he left, Tommy came up to her.

'They're leaving the country,' Tommy said, nodding towards the Grimwigs. 'That solicitor, Poulter, he gave them steamer tickets, to someplace called Buenos Aires. That's in the Argentine. A family room for four and a separate first-class berth. Her, the kids and a servant—some kind of bodyguard, the solicitor said. Nice to be rich, ain't it?'

'A bodyguard doesn't surprise me, with all those people after them. He didn't do a good job at the theatre, though.'

'They're going this weekend.'

'So soon?' Mary said, worried.

Wasn't Dora Grimwig concerned, even curious, about the man who murdered her husband, that she should leave the country so quickly? Surely, she'd want to see him arrested and tried? The Grimwigs were odd people, but this decision was strange. Why would the widow go when her victory over Mary, her revenge taken out on Archie, was so near completion?

Mary's worries, though, were about what Mrs Grimwig's decision meant for Archie. It was frustrating not to be able to do anything to help him. But if they left, then, what chance would she have to prove what they'd done?

Then she wondered how the widow would be allowed to leave the country at such short notice, only to realise that the authorities probably didn't know about her plans.

When she mentioned it to Tommy, the boy said, 'Fleeing the debtors, I shouldn't wonder.'

He showed her a paragraph in the newspaper as reported by Sydney Bottle. It announced the postpone-ment of the Earl of Marchmere's civil action against Mr Grimwig, due to be heard that Friday. New papers would have to be drawn up by the plaintiff for the action to proceed, no doubt citing Dora Grimwig as the defendant. That would take time, and by then, Mrs Grimwig would be gone.

'No wonder she wanted the funeral quick,' Mary said.

She raked her fingers through her hair. Too many things troubled her.

FOLLOWING MRS GRIMWIG

MARY WAS ABOUT to set out for home, when Tommy pointed to where Mrs Grimwig and her children were waiting on the pavement across the road. A large, enclosed black carriage, drawn by two horses, pulled up. The blinds were pinned down. The carriage could easily accommodate a party of six if necessary. The driver caught her attention. She'd seen him only once before, and then briefly. That was many months ago. She remembered his wild eyes. It was he who drove the hansom that tried to run her down in Oxford Street not long after Mr Grimwig accused her of theft. Afterwards she saw Grimwig's butler, Mr Boots, and an assassin she later knew as Black Bob, watching her on the corner of the street the driver turned down.

The carriage pulled away. A morbid curiosity kept her looking. The carriage went no more than fifty yards before stopping. A small, wiry man with prominent bushy eyebrows wandered out of a shadowy doorway towards it.

'Isn't he that copper that Mr Baynes is looking for?' Tommy asked.

Mary nodded.

A feminine hand holding several pieces of white paper appeared. The man took the papers. Raising his hat, he gave something of a servile bow. He folded and slipped the papers inside the breast pocket of his coat, turned and left.

'What was all that about?' Tommy's brow crinkled.

Mary gave him a look of disbelief, only for the noise of Mr Poulter leaving the coroner's building to draw her attention. He was arguing some legal points with another man. Her vision slipped back to the carriage. It was travelling slowly, at a fast walking pace only. She grabbed Tommy's wrist.

'Come on,' she said.

'Where?'

She pointed with a firm chin. 'The carriage. Get across the road, don't lose it.'

For a second he hesitated. 'Follow it, you mean?' he asked.

Mary gave him a stern look and Tommy forced a tight, awkward smile.

'This ain't no game, is it?'

'I want to know where she goes,' Mary said and started off.

The boy clenched his jaws. Stumbling, still hesitant, he scrambled across the street, peeping several times towards Mary as if to ask if she was serious.

The carriage moved at a leisurely pace, and the occupants were in no hurry. At a trot, Mary and Tommy could keep up. Still, someone running behind a carriage could easily be construed as what it was. She hoped Tommy had the good sense to keep to the shadows as much as possible, just as she was doing, and to walk when necessary.

Her mind, though, was alive with questions. She knew something was not right. The bribe the policeman took was at the forefront of her thoughts. That and recalling the annoyed look on Baynes's face, wondering where his junior had gotten to. And something else troubled the inspector, she was certain.

By degree, their surroundings changed. The larger, splendid houses from around the coroner's court gave way to darker, older, less well-kept buildings. Their obvious neglect suggested poverty. The rank miasma of sewerage coloured the air. Soon the streets narrowed and the houses, neither small nor large, leant closer over them. The carriage wound its way along, the wheels crunching against the stone underneath, the horses' clip-clopping rhythmically keeping up a constant unhurried pace.

Despite the icy cold, before long Mary was sweating. They were entering Rotherhithe, a disreputable place as any that she knew to exist in London. She could not help thinking that this was where Dickens's Bill Sykes met his end, above the close tenement streets, amongst the putrefying filth and the stagnant waste they were walking past and through. It was an unwelcomed thought from a mind that refused to be stilled.

If this was where the Grimwigs now lived, then how far the mighty had fallen. Rotherhithe, where the stink of the river filled the air, was as far removed from their once splendid home in Regent's Park as one could wish. The pleasant odours of Christmas cheer never came here. This was someplace Mary would not choose to live.

Unconsciously, she and Tommy had fallen into a pattern. When she trotted on one side of the street, he fell back and walked nonchalantly, albeit quickly, on the other. At an unseen signal, he would trot up and take the lead, giving her a chance to walk and get her breath back. In this way, they alternated until, after a while, the carriage drew up outside a taller building than the rest on the shadowy side of the street.

Mary couldn't see the occupants dismount from her vantage point, but knew they went inside. Now that she knew where the Grimwigs lived, she was unsure of herself. Some second sense made her follow them, an instinct only, or a distrust of people that she needed to know more about. *Scientia potential est!* Those were the major's words, and the more she knew, the safer she'd feel.

As the carriage moved away, Tommy slipped back from across the street. He was smiling. His fears and doubts passed with the excitement of doing what he always wanted to do. More so, as he had been successful. No one noticed them as they trailed their quarry to its lair.

'Did you see them go inside?' Mary asked. Her complexion was florid with her efforts and she wiped the perspiration away from her brow with a handkerchief.

The boy nodded. 'All five of them.'

'Five?'

'Her and the kids and a bloke as well—that body-guard the solicitor spoke about, I reckon. I didn't get a chance to see him proper. It was too dark and he was too quick for me.'

Mary slipped back and leant against the wall. She raised her head into the air and closed her eyes tightly, gritting her teeth in annoyance.

'I've been a fool, Tommy,' she whispered. She glanced idly towards Grimwig's house and bit her lip. She lifted her head and gently banged the back of it several times lightly against the wall she was leaning on.

The boy looked at her confused.

'Well, Mary, I didn't want to say anything, but the major says there should always be a plan—'

'A separate first-class room on the steamer. For a bodyguard? Stupid Finch,' she muttered.

The thoughts that ruminated in her head needed confirmation. She eyed the dark windows of Grimwig's house. 'I have to see inside. I need to know something.'

Tommy shook his head. 'No way am I going in there.' He was adamant. His fears returned. 'I mean, if we're caught!' His eyes dropped in embarrassment. 'I ain't afraid,' he said quickly, and looked up sheepishly.

Tommy Tiggs was no coward. He'd insisted on entering her lodging rooms first, fully aware that an assassin might be lurking behind the door, and done so without hesitation. He'd been as brave as a lion. But ever since that day when they dismissed her, Mary understood what the Grimwigs were capable of. He was afraid, just the same way she was, not by getting caught by the police, awful enough as that would be, but of Dora Grimwig. After all, the Grimwigs tried to murder her several times already, so why shouldn't he be worried?

The house, a tenement, was squeezed between dark buildings on either side. Mary's gaze slipped to those windows overlooking Grimwig's house from across the street. With luck, they may give her a glimpse inside. As she scanned them, thinking about how best she could get inside one, her eyes fell on Absalon Furie. The giant was standing at the opposite end of the street, in the shadows that could barely conceal him. The Imp, George Bradley's description of his companion, was walking towards him. For a moment, she wondered if they'd followed her just as she'd followed the Grimwigs. In that same moment, she wondered if he'd seen them. Noticing that they'd arrived from the opposite direction, she was relieved, but more so when it was clear that they'd not seen her. Furie and the Imp dropped deeper into the shadows and vanished.

Any thoughts she had about spying on the Grimwig also vanished. Being caught by Dora Grimwig was one thing, but being caught by Furie… She felt Tommy's trembling hand on her arm. Like him, she now wanted to go. She made a mental note. There had to be another way to get into the Grimwig's house, an alleyway, perhaps, that lay somewhere in the shadow where Furie went. Dora Grimwig would not want the leg-breakers to be seen entering the house from the street. Mary knew what she had to do.

'Tommy, let's go back. There's a copper I need to see.'

The boy exhaled with relief.

❧ 21 ☙

CHARING CROSS MORGUE

MARY HAD KNOWN Constable O'Connor for less than a year. In that time, he'd wrongfully arrested her for the theft of Mrs Grimwig's jewels; he'd helped her solve the case of the Grey Lady, who tried to murder her mistress, Mrs Grady; and he'd helped her find her brother. She, on the other hand, helped him lose his promotion. His newly-acquired sergeant stripes were barely a few days old before they were removed from him, and she was the cause. Nevertheless, he didn't blame her, and they remained firm friends.

Leaving Tommy to go back to Deacon House, Mary found O'Connor exiting Bow Street police station, bound for his beat in Soho. His demeanour was dour. He clearly had been following Archie's case. Mary braced herself for yet more bad news. It seemed each day, more nails

178

were being driven into Archie's coffin—the Grimwigs would not let go of their vitriol.

'Some IOUs were found bearing Archie's signature,' O'Connor said with a shake of his head. 'It's not looking good.'

Mary's heart sank. She struggled to get her breath and sat heavily on a bench in Covent Garden market. Now she understood the look on Inspector Baynes's face at the inquest and what it was he didn't tell her.

'Where were they found?'

'In the back of Zielinski's ledger. Inspector Baynes's junior, Sergeant Quist, discovered them this morning.' Mary's heart sank lower still. How convenient, she thought. She wanted to tell O'Connor she'd seen Quist take a bribe from Mrs Grimwig only a few hours earlier, but without proof, it would be pointless. So, he was helping the Grimwigs enact their revenge on her. Was that payment for the IOUs or for something else?

'What does it all mean?' she asked.

She looked up pleadingly, hoping against hope that he would assuage her fears. Instead, O'Connor seemed to sink back into himself.

'The Crown is building a hanging case. It's like a jig-saw puzzle. Each new piece adds to it, and each new piece is bad news for Archie. The Crown's contention will be that he killed Zielinski to retrieve the IOUs.'

'They're going to hang Archie, aren't they?' she said softly.

O'Connor sighed. Again, he shook his head sadly. 'His chances aren't good. Not good at all. And the IOUs —' He didn't finish; he didn't need to.

Mary gritted her teeth and clenched her fists in anguish. 'This is Grimwigs' doing,' she snarled. 'He set Archie up. You have to believe me.'

'It's not me that needs convincing, Mary. It'll be a jury of twelve.'

This was what Druze said. He too feared some connection being found between Archie and Zielinski. Brick by brick, the Crown was building a wall around her friend. Stick by stick, they were building his gallow.

'I…' she hesitated and swallowed nervously, partially in fear for what she was about to ask, and partially remembering a time, not so long ago, when she was tasked with such a chore. 'Please, I want to see Mr Grimwig's body… he's in the morgue and I don't know how and where and—'

'Why?' O'Connor asked.

Mary just looked at him. His expression was one of curiosity mixed with concern. A second later, he nodded. She reached out an arm to hold his, remembering her part in his demotion only that summer.

'I-I don't want to get you into any trouble,' Mary said.

He winked. A smile came to his face that Mary knew hid his worries. 'Didn't I tell you? Trouble's my middle name. Let me tell Harry where I'll be so he can cover my beat. It's lucky I know you, Mary Finch. Others I'd give short shrift to, and be happy to do it.' As he arose, he took a deep breath. 'It'll not be pleasant. Are you sure you want to do this?'

'I have to, for Archie's sake.'

'When we're there, just leave the talking to me,' he said.

It was a silent journey; Mary's thoughts were dark and fearsome, her stomach knotted, and at other times, it bubbled nervously.

When they arrived at the hospital, she waited a few minutes as O'Connor made the arrangements.

The corridor to the morgue led them deep into the cellars beneath Charing Cross Hospital. It was a dark, cold, echoey place that reeked of carbolic. She held her breath. It was the same odour she remembered in the room Professor Cavendish occupied, somewhere above them, the last time she was here. Mary shivered. The other smell, at the time, was of violets.

The grey-faced attendant escorting them had sunken cheeks that gave him a skeletal look. He carried his own atmosphere about with him, a dark air that somehow suited his occupation with the dead.

He took them to a large, white-tiled room and asked them to wait.

The room was sparse but for a large table in the middle. A rack of lights hung over it. On a wall was a deep ceramic sink. On another wall, there were shut cabinets, but for one. She glimpsed inside and quickly turned away in horror at the implements on display. Mary edged away from a drain she was standing near as the butterflies in her stomach took flight and circled restlessly, hoping they would not escape. She noticed O'Connor was standing still and calm, rocking on his heels. She was glad he was there with her. Even so, Mary fidgeted and bit the corner of her bottom lip continuously, trying to make sense of her emotions.

A few minutes passed so slowly that Mary might have thought they were hours before a pair of swing doors barged open and the grey-faced attendant appeared, wheeling a trolley. A pristine white sheet covered a body. He stopped in front of them and respectfully stepped back.

O'Connor took a deep breath.

'You sure you want to do this, Mary?' he asked. 'The bullet would have done an awful lot of damage.'

Mary shook her head, but gave him a look as if to say she had to.

The policeman slowly and carefully lifted the sheet from around the dead man's head. As he did, the corpse's arm slipped off the edge and Mary jumped as it brushed her dress. She saw his completely tanned forearm, hand and fingers. The fingers tips were blackened. She drew her gaze up to his face. When she saw it, her world spun. A creeping darkness clouded her eyes. It closed out her vision and she fainted.

She was looking up at an ornate ceiling, and the buzz of conversation and the bustle of bodies surrounded her. In a corner, there was a Christmas tree. Ribbons were wrapped around it and baubles hung from the branches. Several small children were ogling it, their faces rapt as they chatted and laughed merrily. She was surrounded by natural light, flooding in from a wall of windows. From the street beyond came the soft sounds of a Christmas carol being sung. A bewitching boy soprano was singing *Stille Nacht.* For a moment, she thought she was in heaven.

The pungent odour of ammonia made her screw up her nose in disgust. She realised where she was, lying uncomfortably on a hard-wooden bench in the front reception of the Charing Cross Hospital.

O'Connor was smiling happily at her.

'Not as tough as you'd like everyone to believe, are you, Mary?' he said, amused. She smiled back shyly. 'Don't worry. I lost my stomach the first time I saw a dead body.'

'You didn't faint, though. Was that in Afghanistan?' Mary asked, remembering he was once a soldier.

He nodded. 'A long time ago, and plenty of dead bodies since—and *no*, no fainting.'

She shuffled upright and curled her nose. The tart odour of smelling salts remained. Her memory returned.

'Did you see his fingers?' she asked O'Connor. 'Mr Grimwig was heavily tanned, he wore several rings the last time I saw him—'

'No. Can't say I noticed that,' the policeman said. His eyes were fixed on her. She knew why. He probably gathered her when she swooned, and no doubt, he was still worried about her. She had to focus, otherwise her imagination would overwhelm her and she might faint again. She took a deep breath to compose herself.

'His face...' No, she couldn't do this. She closed her eyes, wishing what she saw would vanish, the damage the bullet had done was extensive. 'You've seen Mr Grimwig—' She was pleading with O'Connor.

'I can't swear it was him, if that's what you mean,' he said knowing exactly what she meant. 'I only ever saw him that once, and with the extent of the wound...' He shook his head. 'You knew him better.'

Mary dithered. 'With the wound, I can't be certain if it was him.'

'The widow is.' Inspector Baynes, standing behind her, placed a hand on her shoulder that made her jump. 'As are some of his... *friends,* shall we call them? Who are we to contradict such assuredness?' Before she could speak, Baynes continued. 'He had Grimwig's wallet, wore his pins and jewels, was the same height, build, wore the same clothes, combed his black hair the same way, had the same carnation in his lapel, but we both know, don't we, Miss Finch, it is not James Grimwig lying down there.' He flicked his head to where the basement would be.

'He didn't have tan lines on his fingers where he wore his rings,' Mary said.

'Ah! You noticed.'

'But if you knew—' Mary said.

'As I said, who are we to contradict the widow's identification? After all, she knew him better than anyone.'

Mary suddenly jumped and glanced around in trepidation.

'Quist?' the inspector said, reading her mind. 'He's off chasing a lead that is leading nowhere.'

Mary was quiet. She'd misread the inspector. Dr Watson indicated he was capable enough to give Sherlock Holmes a run for his money. He certainly wasn't a fool, despite his fresh from the county appearance and mannerisms. Like Mr Holmes, he too liked to keep his cards close to his chest.

'The question to answer is,' he mused, and his face brightened as a slow smile came to it, 'where is Mr Grimwig?'

22

THE CONVERSATION
BETWEEN MARY AND BAYNES

'I ASKED Inspector Baynes to meet us here, Mary,' O'Connor explained. 'I suspected you'd be up to something—not that I expected this. I thought he should be here.'

'He's a fine fellow,' Baynes said, defending the constable and slapping him on the back. 'I'd have him as my sergeant in a heartbeat.'

'I seem to recall I held the rank, once, sir,' O'Connor said. He looked airily upwards. Mary's head dropped low. She felt O'Connor's smile before she saw it.

'So, tell me what else you know, Miss Finch. I suspect you are no slouch,' Baynes said. He took out a pipe and filled it with tobacco and eased back against the bench. 'We can share and share alike,' he joked.

Dr Watson told the inspector much of Mary's dealings with the Grimwigs, so there was no need to remind him. She told him about her attackers, suspecting that the Grimwigs were behind them.

'I think they wanted to scare me,' she said. 'He was just playing with me.'

'Cat and mouse? I can see that,' Baynes said. 'Being pushed down a flight of stairs might injure you, but it was unlikely to be fatal. Neither would the cut, but it would be painful.'

'And the man on Westminster Bridge had ample opportunity to fling me into the Thames. He too was toying with me.' She knew that now. 'But I don't know why Furie interfered.'

'To make sure he didn't kill you—that would spoil the game,' O'Connor said.

'But the cat always kills the mouse when he's had enough of the sport,' Baynes added.

Mary sat back heavily. She wrapped her arms about herself as if cold. 'He wouldn't do it until Archie was hung, would he Mr Baynes? He'd have wanted me to know there was nothing I could have done to prevent it, and then the game would be over.'

'That would be my assessment.' Baynes puffed on his pipe and chewed the mouthpiece. 'As the constable said, Furie's intervention was probably based on his belief that your attacker was going to spoil Grimwig's fun, and that would never do.'

She reached inside her bag and took out the two ticket stubs from the pantomime she and Tommy attended.

'All my cleverness is worth nothing,' she said ruefully. She threw the stubs on the small table in front of them. 'These were sent to me.'

'Anonymously?' he asked.

Mary nodded and Baynes gave her a curious look. He picked up the ticket stubs and contemplated it for a moment.

'Ah! I see. He needed an audience, someone who knew him.' The inspector continued to surprise her.

'Me.'

'And Tommy Tiggs. So, he sent you these.'

'I thought at first they were from my employers,' Mary said, reluctant to mention who they were. 'Or maybe I was meant to think they were a Christmas present from a friend. I don't know.' She shrugged. 'But he needed me there, someone who knew him well. Firstly, to boast to me about what he'd done, knowing I could do nothing about it, and then to be a witness to his murder.'

Baynes nodded in agreement.

'It was a play, a performance, for me and those listening,' Mary continued. 'He must have had an accomplice to conceal a dead body dressed like him in the alleyway. At the interval, his accomplice pretended to be one of Grimwig's angry victims. He drags him into the doorway where they were hidden, a shot is fired and a body is found.'

'Then Grimwig and his accomplice exit stage left. Or

more precisely, through the flats behind the archway. Not pursued by a bear,' Baynes chuckled to himself.

'But he would have had to make sure Mary was there, at that precise moment,' O'Connor said.

'I think our Mr Grimwig would be clever enough to have contrived a way,' Baynes said. 'As such, *she* was there, and, afterwards, once the widow identified the corpse as her husband...'

'Who would question her, she should know him, after all,' Mary finished his sentence.

'Who indeed?' he said.

Mary closed her eyes remembering the event. It happened so quickly and so unexpectedly; she was taken completely by surprise. 'But I saw something, Inspector. It didn't make sense...' She looked around her, rubbed her neck and squinting her eyes almost closed. 'The body was awkward...'

'Stiff?' Baynes advanced.

Mary's eyes opened. 'Yes!' She clearly saw the hospital porters struggling with the corpse.

'And it struck you as strange?' Baynes wore a shallow smile.

'Stupid of me.' Mary heaved a breath.

'Don't be harsh on yourself, Miss Finch. You're not expected to know such things.'

'But I do. Rigor Mortis sets in hours after death—'

'Not the half-hour between the shot and me arriving,' Baynes confirmed, 'but perhaps in between the start of the performance and the end of the first act. And how are you familiar with such a condition, Miss Finch?'

'Dr Watson,' Constable O'Connor answered. 'And that Sherlock Holmes as well, no doubt.'

'Ah!' Baynes nodded.

'But did no one hear the shot that actually killed Mr Grimwig's double?' she asked.

'Apparently not. It may have been muffled somehow. Who knows?'

'I wonder if the man knew his part in the drama?' O'Connor said.

'Really, constable, and I thought you might be my sergeant,' Baynes joked.

'You know what I mean, sir,' said O'Connor, and Baynes smiled a yes.

'But why didn't you say or do something when Mrs Grimwig identified the body?' Mary asked.

'You are clever enough to know the answer, I am sure.'

'The play, it needed to be acted out.'

Baynes nodded, his face was bright like that of a little boy with a secret. 'There was no point interrupting it before its conclusion, if we are to discover all of its purpose.'

'Then you know there's a connection between Archie and Grimwig?'

'Suspect, Miss Finch. Suspect! And I'll warrant that if Mr Grimwig knew that his game had been discovered, you might well be dead by now. Grimwig wouldn't wait for Archie's trial. When did you guess Grimwig was still alive?'

'Not until I saw the body in the morgue, not for certain. But when Tommy Tiggs saw their solicitor give them steamer tickets for South America, that's when I first suspected,' she said and Baynes's eyes rose sharply to meet hers.

'Indeed. That I did not know.'

'They're planning to leave soon. They have a family room for four on the steamer as well as a single room in first-class.'

'Ah! I see. The single room puts a new complexion on things.' He clutched his chin thoughtfully. 'But why leave so soon?' His eyes narrowed and then twinkled. A thin smile curled the corner of his mouth.

'Debtors!' Mary said before he could speak.

'With Grimwig *dead,* they will seek reimbursement from her,' Baynes said. 'By the end of next week, there will be a surfeit of legal writs issued against the good widow and the dead man's estate.'

'Only if they can catch her,' O'Connor added and Baynes chuckled.

'And that Sergeant Quist,' Mary said. 'I can't be sure, I wasn't close enough, but I saw him take money from Mrs Grimwig—'

'After the inquest. Yes. He said a man wanted to see me with urgent information. It turned out to be a wild goose chase. He wanted me out of the room so Poulter could make his application for the body to be released. Quist knew I would object. He thought he was being clever. I would have had to object if I was there. It would have been odd if I did not. And that would have raised suspicions with the Grimwigs. So, it was a good thing that I wasn't there.'

Mary's head snapped up. 'Cremation!'

'Yes, Miss Finch, I see we are riding the same train.' He rubbed his palms together, vigorously. 'No one would be able to contradict the widow's identification once the body is cremated.'

'And you let them believe that their scheme was working. But what about Archie?' Mary asked.

'This doesn't change anything as far as he is concerned,' Baynes said sadly.

'But Grimwig framed Archie,' Mary said. She'd seen a light at the end of a tunnel only for the inspector to shake his head and extinguish it.

'Whether he did or did not, needs to be proved. Apart from you, there are no other connections to the two cases. And these IOUs, is yet another nail…' He didn't need to add, in Archie's coffin.

She sagged inwardly. Grimwig's revenge was being heaped onto her best friend. If he succeeded, she'd live her life knowing Archie's execution would have been her fault for crossing the blackmailer and making an enemy out of him. Even if they caught Mr Grimwig, he wouldn't admit to setting up Archie. Why should he? What had he to lose? You can't hang a man for murder twice, and the body in the morgue was exactly that—murder, as surely as it was with Janusz Zielinski.

'About Mr Quist,' O'Connor said sheepishly. He took a deep, worried breath. 'Am I right to assume he's crooked?

'You have put it mildly in polite company,' Baynes said.

'It's just, I saw him before I saw you.'

'Constable! You did not—'

'Yes, sir, I did. I told him that Mary and I were coming to the morgue and he should inform you to meet us here. Only, I saw you soon after speaking to him. If I had known otherwise…'

Inspector Baynes raised his hand to say he understood. 'Well, that does put the cat amongst the pigeons,' he said.

23

A FATEFUL DECISION

INSPECTOR BAYNES'S face looked dark as they parted company. Mary understood it all too well. He wanted more time to allow the game to play out—*to give the widow sufficient rope to hang herself*. Now that the scheme had been discovered, the risen from the dead Mr James Grimwig would try to flee, but not before directing his ire towards her.

'You go home and stay home, is my advice,' Baynes said. 'Lock the doors and make sure you know the person knocking before you let them in.'

'We should give her some protection,' Constable O'Connor said.

'I'll have frequent patrols around your lodgings, Miss Finch.'

'Are you going to arrest Mrs Grimwig?' Mary asked.

'As soon as I can organise the men and before they

have time to fly.' Like the inspector, Mary knew that there were others like Sergeant Quist in the force. Money was their master, and they would gravitate inexorably to where he could find it the most. He would have to choose his men carefully. A mischievous twinkle sparkled in his eyes. 'We shall do the deed when the *iron tongue of midnight tolls twelve*, as the good bard might put it.'

Mary drew her coat tighter around her shoulders. A light snow was falling. As she left the two policemen on the steps of Charing Cross Hospital, she'd have wished them to move swifter. But she knew only too well what needed to happen. He would have to apply for a warrant, then vet and organise the raiding party. That would take time as it would have to be done in secrecy.

Anxious to get home, Mary hailed a hackney, then she waved it away with an apology. Her mind wouldn't be stilled, and her frustration needed venting, and a swift walk would suffice both.

Christmas was less than a week away. London held its breath in expectation. Each shop she passed displayed some decoration. On each door it seemed was hung a fir and holly wreath; fir cones and red ribbon adorned them. Carols were in the air. Children were running about, peering through frosted toyshop windows, anxiously, happily, expectantly, while their mothers walked beside them, carrying boxes wrapped in brightly patterned paper. The church clocks tolled, marking the hours away, bringing Christmas a step nearer with each chime. Good

Saint Nicholas was about, and Jack Frost was busy nipping noses on a bitterly cold day.

At another time, she would be happy. Today, there was no Christmas cheer in her heart. Mr Grimwig was an evil, bitter man, a viper whose bite was fatal. She was sure that if he himself hadn't murdered Janusz Zielinski, then he'd had an associate do it. Just as surely was his involvement in the death of the man who posed as him in a dark archway near the Theatre Royal, of that she was sure. She glanced around nervously. Through the light snow she expected to see his man, Absalon Furie, dark and menacing, following her.

A thin mist hovered over the Thames as she crossed Westminster Bridge. She stopped briefly and glanced across the river, remembering the summer. Mr Holmes's brother, Mycroft, said what a fine view it was towards Charing Cross from there. It was from that pier below where her own brother departed for Germany. At the time she thought all her troubles were over. She felt free. A change was coming to her and she was carried forward by the tide it brought. Her life was set to be different.

Now Archie, her best friend, was paying for her past. If the law did not hang him, as Mr Druze indicated, then they would lock him away for a very long time indeed. For once, she felt powerless. As clever as she thought herself, she didn't know what to do.

Tommy Tiggs was waiting by the door of her lodgings. He blew a smoky breath into his gloved hands and stamped his feet to keep them warm. His face brightened when he noticed her.

'Blimey, it's nippy today,' he said.

'How long you been here?' Mary asked. The boy looked frozen.

'Bleedin' hours it seems.' He shivered with the cold. 'The major's fuming. He expected to see you back at the house. Mr Bradley sent me to warn you and see how you was doing.'

'You told George about us going to Rotherhithe?'

Tommy nodded, his teeth chattering.

'Come on up. Let's get you warmed up a bit. You eaten? I ain't and I'm famished.'

Once in her rooms, she lit the fire, and as she prepared sandwiches and tea, she told him about going to Charing Cross Hospital and what happened. His eyes widened in amazement.

'You saw him, that Mr Grimwig, I mean that man impersonating him, who was shot, you know, shot in the... Blimey!' He gaped.

Mary did not mention she fainted, but explained what she and Inspector Baynes discussed. At the end, Tommy Tiggs sat back, impressed.

'And you're a girl as well,' he said.

'What's that got to do with anything?' Mary huffed.

'I mean...' he fell silent, as if scolded. 'Blimey!' His eyes looked her up and down. She was barely taller than him, a few years older, and a lot cleverer, he admitted to her.

'It's only because I'm friends with people like Sherlock Holmes and Dr Watson, and know Inspector Lestrade and Mr Gregson,' Mary said, trying to spare the boy's blushes as best she could. 'I just listen when they speak and try to remember what they say.'

His face drooped.

'And you will too, learning from the major and George and the rest in Deacon House,' she said kindly. 'And trust me, seeing a dead body ain't no picnic.' She shivered somewhat dramatically and saw Tommy's protective instincts awake.

'Here, lets's not talk anymore about it, otherwise you won't get any sleep tonight,' he said.

Mary sat back and warmed her hands by the fire.

'I ain't sleeping tonight, anyway,' she said. She sighed heavily and gazed into the flames. 'Tommy, I know it's stupid, but I need to be there when Inspector Baynes goes to the Grimwig's house.'

Tommy gave her a doubtful stare.

'I'm not gonna feel safe until I know they've got him and he's behind bars,' she said. 'And I've got to see that for myself.'

'And you might be able to help Archie as well.' He nodded his head. 'Well, if you're going, so am I.'

'No, I can't ask you that.'

She looked at him, a serious stare and he still nodded his head.

'You ain't. The major says I'm to look out for you and that's what I'll be doing, my job.' He puffed himself up and sat upright. His mouth firmed and he clenched his jaws determinedly. His eyes narrowed into a steely stare.

'What about your mum?' Mary asked.

'Mum knows I sometimes have to work late at a moment's notice.' He looked away quickly, and Mary knew it was to hide the lie.

She warmed to Tommy that first day when he made a joke about what the major said. He wanted to get ahead, not unlike her. In the short time she had known him, she considered him a friend. She leant over and gave him a hug, and Tommy blushed scarlet.

'B-blimey! Your f-fire's warm, ain't it,' he stammered. 'I-I don't suppose you got any milk?'

'On the window ledge,' Mary said and hurried to get it and give the boy a chance to relax.

When she returned with a glass of cold milk, Tommy was himself again.

'We better have a rest before then.' She checked her watch. Six o'clock. If they left by eleven, that'd give them plenty of time. 'Have a kip on the couch. It ain't that comfortable, but it's better than the chair. I'll get you a blanket. I'll have a lie down myself. Help yourself to what there is to eat. I'm sure you'll be missing a good feed from your mum tonight.'

'Shepherd's Pie night,' he licked his lips.

'Eileen, Mrs Grady's cook, would make stew on a night like this. Hot and filling, with dumplings and potatoes and carrots and chicken and… Cor! Listen to that, that's me stomach gurgling. I miss her cooking.'

'You going there for Christmas?' he asked and Mary nodded. 'I bet she'll feed you up, just like mum does with us.'

'Who's us?' she asked.

'Effie, that's me little sister, and Harry, me brother. I'm the eldest. Mum and dad makes five.'

'What does dad do?'

'He works in one of those Gentlemen's club in Mayfair. You see, dad used to be a corporal in the army and he saved the life of this general so-and-so, and it was him that got him his job—and mine for that matter.' Tommy giggled. 'You should see dad when he's dressed in the club's uniform. What a sight! Looks like General bleedin' Gordon, he does, with his sashes and braids.'

She envied Tommy his family, his mum and dad, and his time with them, time she never had with hers. He was smiling happily, thinking about them. The Dibbles became her family when Grandpa Dibble took her in without a second thought that day so many years ago. She owed them their kindness more than she could ever repay.

Poor Archie. She was why he was in jail, about to be tried for murder, and on the basis of the evidence against him, found guilty and hanged. She got to her feet, all of the sudden tired. With everything that had happened she'd not been sleeping well. Then she felt it: her fears and how less sure she was of herself than ever before.

'Tommy. Thanks,' she said, grateful for his company. Then the smile left her face and her expression hardened. 'Inspector Baynes won't be happy to see me there. Nor will my friend Constable O'Connor.' Grimly determined, she faced Tommy. 'Well, they'll just have to be unhappy, won't they, because Archie is the nearest thing I've got to family since Danny left, and I won't see him hung—I'm going.'

❦ 24 ❧

TO ROTHERHITHE

THE CHURCH CLOCK chimed quarter to eleven as Mary and Tommy emerged from her blackened terraced house and hurried away eastwards towards Rotherhithe. On a bitterly cold, starlit night, she and Tommy moved swiftly through streets glazed with snow, a mild dusting that faithfully recorded each step they made along their way. At this late hour the streets were deserted and fit only for those creatures of the night who contemplated dark deeds. Pursuing the midnight hour, they travelled in mute silence.

A cold horror invaded her bones as Mary thought she heard the disquieting pattering of footsteps, like an echo, behind her. She shivered and turned in terror, but saw nothing. By now, she knew Grimwig would have suspected his ruse had been discovered. Quist would have seen to that. Baynes's words came back to fill her mind with dread: *the cat always kills the mouse when it has had enough of the game.* She could sense it: the game was coming to an end.

Passing the Elephant and Castle, they hurried down the Old Kent Road and into Bermondsey. Slipping through dark, deserted streets, under railway arches, and through dank, depressing alleys where the homeless slept in scant comfort on such a night as this, she and Tommy raced along, chasing their frosted breaths, until finally, unseen, they entered Rotherhithe.

It was in just such streets as these that she once found herself, the night she ran away from Mrs Fortesque. For a short time, at ten-years-old, she too was once like these vagabonds, inhabiting doorways, nooks, and crannies, alone and afraid. By the grace of God and the goodness of the Dibbles, she was saved.

In the morning, these mazes of streets, close and narrow, would throng with the poorest of people. They would pass shops selling the meanest of provisions, and the unemployed would jostle, cheek by jowl, with the commonest of labourers. The most ragged of children and the riff-raff of the river, would be cast up here on the high tide water mark that were the streets of Rotherhithe. But tonight, Mary delighted in its emptiness, knowing her quarry would not be able to hide and be lost amongst the crowds.

Panting from their exertions, they rested for a few minutes in a doorway and out of a numbing breeze blowing in from across the river, to catch their breaths once more. She blew into her closed palms to warm her icy fingers, then wiped her sleeve across her red, dripping nose. She listened intently. Straining her ear against the silence, she heard them: the footsteps following her. She heard them fall away to be swallowed by the cold night air, and then a heavy silence, broken only by her rasping breath. Somewhere in the shadows, someone was stalking her. Mary felt his eyes watching her. He was waiting patiently for his chance.

Tommy had not heard them; the boy was red-faced and puffing, and for a moment she feared for them both. Her fears quickly passed when she saw several policemen walking silently to where she knew was Grimwig's house. A shout and they would descend on whomever it was dogging their steps. Inspector Baynes and Constable O'Connor would be nearby. But perhaps their stalker had seen them as well, and knew, he, too, must be stealthy. She didn't care for the analogy, but it was a game of cat and mouse after all.

'Let's go,' she whispered to Tommy.

The boy nodded and arose with her.

They slipped quietly around the corner. In front of them were several policemen waiting patiently. Their lamps were covered so no light could betray their presence. They hung back inside the shadows, hiding as best as possible. At the far end of the street stood several more, Inspector Baynes prominent amongst them. Under his direction, they moved silently and purposefully, slowly edging up the street to Grimwig's door, while several slipped into the alleyway behind the house.

A hand fell on Mary's shoulder, and she jumped, but stifled her scream.

'What are you doing here?' Constable O'Connor whispered.

'I had to be here,' she whispered back.

'And how's this gonna help Archie? That's who you're here for, ain't you?'

'You know I am. And I don't know. I just need to be here. I ain't leaving.'

'No, I can see that. But you're staying here, is that clear?' O'Connor said, and he pulled her back a little to make his point. 'Who's your friend?'

'Tommy Tiggs,' Mary said and the boy smiled at the policeman.

'You keep her here, Tommy. *Is that clear?*'

With that, O'Connor took his place ahead of the men and slowly walked forward. By then, Baynes had reached the Grimwig's door. He banged on it with his closed fist, the thumps echoing along the street. A few seconds later, he thumped it again, louder, and shouted: 'Police! Let us in.' A heavy silence followed before he did it a third and a fourth time, louder on each occasion.

From inside the house came a muffled disturbance. Lights sprang up behind several windows. The curtains were drawn back in a few, and Mary saw faces peering out at the policemen surrounding the door. Baynes, by now, had taken to continually banging on the door with his fist, shouting and demanding entry.

A window flew up, and Mrs Grimwig leant out. 'What do you want?' she bellowed.

The inspector stepped back and into the street to get a better view. Now that he was no longer thumping the door, the whole street was silent. One of the policemen shone his lantern upwards to illuminate the angry, irate face of Dora Grimwig.

'Let us in,' Baynes shouted. 'I have a warrant to search these premises and for the arrest of your husband.'

'My husband is dead, Inspector. Well you know.'

'Madam, I have no inclination to parley,' Baynes said, 'and I'd advise you to do the same. This is my warrant.' He shook a folded piece of paper at her, his face triumphant. 'Now open the door, or we shall open it ourselves?'

'My lawyer shall hear of this,' Mrs Grimwig shouted. Her head twisted around as there came an echoing racket of fists crashing against the backdoor of the house.

'The house is surrounded,' Baynes informed her.

'How dare you disturb a poor widow at this time of the night.'

'Madam, this is folly. Do as I ask.'

The racket elicited an audience. Windows were being unfastened and faces leant out. Doors opened and people, wrapped in coats and blankets, came to stand and gaze in silent curiosity at the commotion taking place in front of Grimwig's house.

'See how ill-treated I am?' Mrs Grimwig implored the gathering crowd. 'My husband, dead these past few days, and my poor children, fatherless—'

'Madam, desist with this foolishness.'

'His funeral is yet to be arranged, and we are set upon by these creatures—'

'Madam, will you let us in or must we force an entry?'

'Damn you!' Mrs Grimwig scowled and lifted her voice to the listening crowd. 'See how tasked we are. See how we are abused—'

'Break it down,' Baynes shouted to his men and stepped out of their way.

Immediately, two policemen charged the door. It resisted them. It was solidly built. They resumed their attack. Behind them gathered the other constables, O'Connor foremost amongst them. With truncheon drawn, like eager greyhounds, they strained at their leashes, anxious to be released, willing their colleagues to break down the door.

Once again, the constables attacked the door, and on the fourth occasion, it splintered off its hinges, the frame splitting and it fell back with a heavy bang inside the building. Without a second's pause, Baynes and his men entered. Very soon, the street outside was empty of policemen. A wailing banshee cry reverberated in the cold night air from within the house.

The sound of heavy footsteps crashing against floorboards and against doors, could be heard from inside. In each and every window, the torches the policemen carried shone a flickering, dancing light against the blinds and net curtains.

Mary stepped into the street to get nearer. The windows of the front room were suddenly ablaze with light, and the occupants of the house could be seen gathered there. She could hear the cries of the triplets and see them clutching each other in the living room.

Soon the ruckus in the house faded away, to be replaced by a heavy silence. Whispers sprang up from around where Mary waited. People now took to standing outside on the pavement, despite the bitter night. Some gathered in groups. With all the policemen now in the house, they watched in fascination the happenings there.

Mary moved into the middle of the road, equally curious, when the sharp sounds of tinkling and a crash from the far end of the street, caught her attention. Glancing there, she saw several people quickly step back and out of the way. Her eyes rose upwards. Three figures were making their way across the top of the roof. As they slipped and slid on the frosty surface, the tiles, masonry and plaster they dislodged swept downwards and crashed onto the pavement.

Mary rushed over to where the tiles had smashed. She

glanced back. The street was empty of policemen, they were all inside Grimwig's house.

'Get Constable O'Connor,' Mary shouted to Tommy.

The boy grabbed her arm. 'Where you going?' he asked.

Mary picked up a large piece of old flaky plaster. She scratched a large arrow onto the wall of the building

'Just get him to follow my trail. Hurry.' Mary took off, leaving Tommy in the middle of the street. 'You're not getting away, if I can help it,' she whispered to herself.

25

BICKERING THIEVES

BY THE TIME she reached the corner of the street, the three figures had vanished from the roof. Mary eased back into the shadows and waited. She scanned the dark empty street ahead of her wondering which house they'd gone into and from which they'd emerge from, because emerge they would. Then she heard the snap of a bolt being drawn, and the complaining creak of hinges of a door swinging open, and she saw them. Mr Grimwig, Sergeant Quist and another man dashed across the road.

Mary followed them as they ran along to another street and slipped around the corner. She scratched an arrow with the plaster across the walls, marking her direction. Then, each time they made a turn, she recorded it on a brick wall or on the pavement where there was one, as she chased after them. The men were heading in a northerly direction. Mary could guess where. The river was nearby.

She considered shouting and raising the alarm, but she was now too far away from Inspector Baynes and his men. She must follow and hope Tommy found the policemen and they were close behind her.

The three men ran silently down twisting streets and passages, getting farther and farther away from where they started. Soon they turned into a small street, no more than an alleyway. She watched them walk ghostly across the alley before entering a door in front of the most rundown building she'd ever seen. A long-abandoned warehouse, it leant awkwardly over the roadway awaiting demolition. The crumbling walls, glassless windows, shattered doorways, lay it open together with the ruptured roof. It was in a condition so destitute that only the desperate would dare enter. Somehow, she knew, this was their destination.

Mary glanced behind her. She couldn't see Tommy or the policemen she sent him to fetch. She didn't know where the building issued out, only that the river was nearby, possibly on the other side. She feared a boat awaited them. Soon they would be gone. She scratched another arrow, hoping Tommy would be quick and her signs noticed.

The roof above the ruin was almost gone. Several beams still spanned the space and the half-moon shone brightly in the frosty air, casting a cold dead light and great swathes of black shadows. The floor was strewn with debris all covered with a dusting of snow. It was here the men stopped; their frosted breaths clear in the night air.

Mary crept into the devastation and carefully picked her way to someplace she could hide. The far wall was collapsed, and the lights of Limehouse twinkled across the quiet river. In the cold light of the moon, the slack waters of low tide revealed the muddy banks of the Thames, glassy and deeply unwelcoming. She heard one of the men curse, and her heart quickened when she realised. The returning tide would take hours to fill the river. Their plan to escape vanished along with the water.

She waited, concealed, ready to follow them if they should leave. But instead, the men were squabbling. Mr Grimwig's voice, foremost and insistent amongst theirs, was raised in a guttural whisper. Mary shivered at hearing it again.

'What the hell do I pay you for?' Grimwig hissed.

'It weren't my fault. Baynes is a clam. I knew nothing about this raid.'

'I reckon he's tumbled you, Quist,' the third man said. 'Why else would he keep you in the dark?'

'I reckon the same,' Grimwig said. He scowled at the policeman and swore under his breath.

'Don't blame me,' Quist replied angrily. 'You should have done for that girl instead of playing games.'

'I'll do for her yet. As soon as that boy hangs.'

'Let's hope you can do a better job than your friends,' the third man said. 'For such hard men, seems they can't handle a fourteen-year-old girl.'

She recognised the third man when the moonlight caught his face. It was he who drove the carriage from the coroners to Rotherhithe. Mary slipped behind a fallen beam resting against the wall. She hunkered down, hoping they'd go their own separate ways. Following Grimwig would be easier than following them all, and it was Grimwig she wanted. As she stole deeper into the shadows, she heard him growl lowly and mumble something she knew was another curse.

'We should split up,' Grimwig said.

'I ain't letting you out of my sight,' the third man said.

'Nor me,' Quist added.

'Well, aren't you a fine trusting pair,' Grimwig said.

'When I get my share, I'll trust you then,' Quist said.

'We want what's owed, Grimwig. Then we can say our farewells.'

'No one gets a penny until I deal with the girl, is that clear?'

'Damn it! Ain't it enough the boy will swing?'

'No, Mr Quist. It ain't. So, make up your minds. If we stays together we'll be caught. Then, see how much money you can spend breaking stones on Dartmoor for the next twenty years.'

'Breaking stones will be the least of your worries.'

Quist scowled. 'They'll hang you for sure, Grimwig, have no doubts about that.'

Grimwig scowled. 'And what do you think will happen to a copper in jail? A bent one at that?'

'All right, shut it,' the third man said. 'We'll split up. Grimwig's right. We'll be safer on our own. Anyways, it's him they're after, more'n us.'

Quist flinched and stared menacingly at both. 'Except I still ain't going until I get a third share of Milverton's stash,' Quist said.

'Then you better make sure I don't hang, because I don't exactly carry it around with me,' Grimwig said. 'But maybe we ought to give Jacko the bigger share. Remember. It was him that broke into Milverton's house the week after he died.'

Quist growled and ground his teeth, recognising Grimwig's taunt. He reached down and wrapped his fingers around a piece of masonry.

'It was Jacko who knew where the old beggar kept his rare stuff, the ones that weren't burned with the rest,' Grimwig continued. 'Jacko I can trust to do a good job, but you Quist...'

Quist flinched. Grimwig had stopped short of calling him useless. He clenched the stone tighter and lifted it up menacingly.

'No one's cheating me, Grimwig. I did my part. I made sure no one saw Jacko. And I did it quickly before anyone could find Milverton's other safe.'

'So, you and Jacko thinks you don't need me?'

'Maybe we don't. Maybe that wife of yours knows where you've hidden it. Maybe if Jacko and me ask her, she'll tell us,' Quist said through clenched teeth.

'And maybe she does and maybe she doesn't. And maybe I'll take it to my grave,' Grimwig said. 'That's a lot of maybes, Quist.'

'I'm willing to take that chance.'

'You'd lose. Me and only me knows where it's hidden.'

'Then maybe I'll just beat it out of you?' Quist showed Grimwig the lump of masonry that he clutched.

Grimwig did not flinch. 'You're all talk, Quist. A mouth only.'

Quist edged closer to Grimwig. 'Let's see what I am—'

'Cut it out, Grimwig,' Jacko said. 'You as well, Quist. Put that down, do you hear me?' He cut a terrible stare at the policeman who, hesitating a second, allowed the lump of masonry to slip from his grasp. 'We're in it together and that's the way of it.'

'Fine,' Quist grunted.

'We'll split and meet at the inn on the Dover Road as planned,' Jacko said.

'Once we're out, I'll double back and get the stuff from the house,' Grimwig said.

'You cheat us,' Quist warned him, 'and I'll see you dead. I swear, I'll see you dead.'

'Not before I kills him first.' Jacko gave Grimwig such a deathly stare that Mary had no doubts he would do exactly what he just promised.

'There's more than enough for the three of us,' Grimwig scoffed. 'But just you remember, I'm the only one who knows where it's hidden. Milverton's rare birds will set us up good, just you see,' he added, seemingly to appease the other two.

Mary shivered. There was a time when Grimwig was top dog, when he had people like Mr Boots and Black Bob working for him, people like Jacko and Quist. How times changed to have them as partners. The three men glared at each other. There was not an ounce of honour amongst thieves, or a thimble full of trust between them.

Slowly, the men turned, ready to leave. They padded lightly toward the opposite side of the building where a section of wall had fallen away. They would follow the river bank eastwards and into the empty streets of Rotherhithe, beyond the waiting police. And then they would split up.

Mary glanced anxiously behind her. There was still no sign of Tommy or O'Connor. She arose, determined to follow Grimwig. As she stood, leaning her weight against the beam she had been hiding behind to steady herself, she felt it shift. It slid off the wall with a howling, scraping noise and crashed to the floor with a bang like a gunshot. Immediately, a flock of pigeons clawed into the air all around her, flapping their wings, blowing debris and dust, clattering into things and themselves, flying in and out of the rafters and beams, circling around her, making the devil's own din.

Mary looked up in horror. The three men turned towards her. Frozen by some spell, they looked at her in total astonishment.

26

AN UNEXPECTED
INTERRUPTION

THEN THE SPELL BROKE.

Immediately, Grimwig edged his way across the debris-covered floor towards her. His eyes narrowed in his dark, angry face. A knot of hard muscle rippled across his jaw. He flung out his hand in a silent order for Quist and Jacko to go to the door and cut off her retreat.

Mary stumbled back until she felt the wall behind her and could go no further. She glanced to her right to see the muddy river, while on her left, Quist and Jacko stood in her way. There was no escape.

'Stay back, you two,' Grimwig growled. 'She's mine.'

'Don't come near me,' Mary shouted.

She reached down and grasped a stout stick, and menaced it at Grimwig. He stopped for a brief moment and hurried forward again. Mary swung the stick, and

Grimwig reached out and grabbed it. He twisted it out of her grip and pushed her back. She crashed against the wall.

'Murder! Murder!' Mary shrieked. 'Help!'

At the same moment, to Grimwig's utter surprise, Mary threw herself at him. Such was the force and the energy of her attack that they both tumbled across the floor. Heedless to the blows, Mary kicked and scratched, all the while her cries of 'Help!' rent the air.

'For God's sake,' Quist shouted, 'shut her up.'

Jacko screamed, 'She'll bring the Devil's own upon us.'

Grimwig, a good deal heavier, brought his advantage to bare. Twisting her around, he pressed her down with his weight. His hand reached out and enclosed her throat. His eyes bulged wide in his dark, demonic face.

'Shut up! Shut up!' he cried. 'Damn you! Shut up!'

Mary gasped a breath and tensed her neck muscles against his choking grip. She reached up and drew long scratches across his face, her nails biting deeply into his flesh and closing his eyes. Grimwig screamed in pain. As his hand came up to prise hers loose, Mary bucked and kicked hard, and he tumbled away.

She scrambled to her feet and fell back once more against the wall. Her legs were shaking, her racing heart almost exploding in her chest. Grimly determined, and roused by her small success, she continued to shout.

'Don't just stand there,' Jacko cried to Quist, 'shut her up!'

Both men edged towards her. Mary's voice fell away. She glared at them and pressed back as far as she could go against the wall. Then her breath caught in her throat when she saw Grimwig rising. The mark of Cain was upon him. His bloody scratched eyes were fixed on her. Within them, she saw all his hatred, his utter contempt for her, his single-minded determination. At that moment, nothing else mattered other than his revenge on the girl he blamed for his misfortunes.

'Leave her be,' Grimwig hissed. 'I ain't done yet.'

He waved Quist and Jacko away. Mary was to be his and his alone. He would brook no interference. He advanced slowly and then, suddenly, rushed her. Of all the cries mortal man could make, none could exceed that which issued from Grimwig's mouth at that instant when he fell on her.

But he'd underestimated his prey. Mary was no longer just the scullery maid he'd once employed. Her confidence had grown and had been tempered by the flames of her resolve. She wouldn't be easily scared and terrorised, a victim of any bully, no matter who it might be. As Grimwig charged, she rushed towards him. Just as his hands went for her throat, she reached out and grasped his coat. Using his momentum, she fell onto her back, pulling him towards her. With a leg extended and pressed into his stomach, she levered and carried him high into the air, just as Miss Danvers taught her. Grimwig flew, head over heels in a cartwheel, crashed into the wall, and crumpled onto the floor. As he landed, there came a sharp, sickening crack and his animal howl of pain.

She scowled at him as he lay writhing in agony.

'Get her,' Quist shouted.

Mary jumped to her feet. She quickly stepped away from Grimwig to give herself room. As she braced for another attack, she saw Absalon Furie. The giant stood as a silent witness behind Quist and Jacko. Near him stood the Imp, who carried an iron pipe in his hand that he whacked dully into the palm of the other one. Her blood ran cold when she saw Furie's lips curl angrily. Her moment of victory was fleeting. She needed to run, just as Archie once advised her to do. But the only way was towards the river, and the outgoing tide left a morass. Even so, her best chance was there, slim as it was.

'Now, now, my good fellows,' Furie spoke, and Quist and Jacko spun around at the sound of his voice. 'Two against one is hardly sport, especially as one is a girl.' Both men gave each other fearful glances. 'And you're forgetting what I told you: she's mine, and mine alone.' He pointed a menacing finger at them. 'You really must listen to me. So perhaps, since you want her so badly, you'd like to try me on for size, first.' Furie balled his fists into great bludgeons.

To Mary's surprise, Jacko launched himself at Furie.

He landed several blows, all to no effect. It looked as if the giant had allowed him that advantage, because in an uncaring wave, he swatted the carriage driver away with contemptuous ease, as one would do to an annoying fly. When Quist tried to bolt, Furie shot out an arm and grasped him. The policeman kicked, and in a fearfully swift motion, Furie reached out and wrapped his hand completely around Quist's ankle like it was a manacle, until his thumb met his fingers.

Furie's face blossomed into a roaring laugh.

With his leg held firmly, all Quist could do to prevent himself from falling was to hop on the other leg. Furie, delighting in the man's predicament, edged him back towards the lip of the wharf. Once there, he leant Quist over the edge, still holding him by his ankle. The policeman found himself balanced on one leg at a forty-five-degree angle, with a drop of twenty feet below him.

Mary was about to rush away, taking advantage of Furie's attention set elsewhere, only to see the Imp blocking her way. He was standing over Jacko, the pipe clutched in his hand. His eyes rose to meet hers.

'And how are you keeping on this fine night, Miss?' He spoke casually and conversationally.

When Grimwig moaned, Furie laughed. 'Not too bad, I should think, Benny?'

The Imp nodded his head. When Jacko tried to squirm away, he tutted, shook his head and pressed a foot on Jacko's chest. As if to warn him that getting up would be a mistake, he slapped the iron pipe into his open palm.

'You're a rare one,' Furie said to Mary. 'Gave me the slip on more than one occasion.'

'You must be getting old,' Benny said.

Again, the bare-knuckle fighter laughed. 'Well, I found her now, haven't I? Just as I said I would,' he growled.

'I ain't scared of you,' Mary barked ferociously and as bravely as she could.

'Ooooh, yes you are,' Furie sneered mockingly, before laughing once more.

'Ooooh, no, she isn't,' the Imp answered teasingly.

'Everyone's afraid of me,' Furie said in a parody of self-importance.

Mary glanced around nervously. The two were behaving as if this were a game, a pantomime, especially as the small man was now whistling and rocking his head from side to side, and doing so quite merrily. She realised that if she made a dash for it, then the Imp was the only one in her way. And she'd rather deal with him than Furie. As she rushed past him, fearing a blow from the iron pipe he carried, to her complete surprise, he did nothing. At that moment, she ran into Inspector Baynes, who reached out and steadied her.

'That'll do, Mr Furie,' Inspector Baynes shouted. He brandished a pistol, aiming at the bare-fist fighter. Behind him came a press of policemen and Tommy Tiggs.

'In a minute, if you please, sir,' Furie said, and bowed his head respectfully. 'The gentleman has some words to say first.'

Mary stood confused, as did the inspector. Tommy came up beside her. In astonished silence, they all watched Furie and Quist.

'It's a long drop, Mr Quist,' Furie said as he peered over the edge. Quist's questioning eyes followed his. 'Aye, you may survive it, but with all that debris down there, sticks and iron and bricks and sharp stones and who knows what else there is there to pierce your flesh, you'll die of blood poisoning before the week's out. And, aye, the good Inspector might shoot me dead, but if he does, I'll drop you. And who knows, I might even contrive to fall on top of you when we reach the bottom. Now speak to the good Inspector before my patience runs out.'

'Damn you to hell, Quist,' Mr Grimwig shouted. He was leaning on his elbow, a snarl of pain and fear on his lips. 'You turn Queen's on me and I'll see you in hell.'

'Aye, Quist,' Furie said. 'And if you don't tell us your tale, you'll get to hell quicker than Grimwig. It's the only chance I'm willing to give you. Confess, man. Turn Queen's evidence, and live.'

O'Connor stepped towards Furie, only for Baynes to reach out an arm and stop him. Then the inspector lowered and holstered his pistol.

'I would like him alive, if that is possible, Mr Furie,' he said calmly.

'Well, since you ask so nicely, I'll try and oblige, sir,' Furie said and nodded politely to the inspector.

'What's going on?' Tommy whispered to Mary.

Mary looked around puzzled. The Imp was still standing over Jacko, still smiling broadly and still whistling, while Furie was still laughing as he suspended Quist over the edge of the wharf by his ankle. It was one of the oddest things Mary had seen in her life.

27

WHAT QUIST SAID

'MR QUIST, do not let me stop you from speaking,' Baynes said.

'I didn't kill no one,' Quist said fearfully. 'You gotta believe me. For God's sake, Mr Baynes, don't let him drop me.'

'There is little I can do about it, Mr Quist,' Baynes said with a shrug.

'Speak to the good Inspector, man.' Furie's eyes lifted and he gazed at the lights on the far shore of the river. 'Benny, where's that we're across from?' he asked.

Looking up, the Imp answered, 'Limehouse.'

Furie nodded, seemingly oblivious to Quist, and whispered wistfully, 'Limehouse. Is that right? It's been a while since I drank in the Old Dog.'

'Well, Quist?' Baynes asked.

'It was Grimwig. It was him, I tells you, it was all his doing.' Quist was almost crying.

Grimwig banged his closed fist in frustration against the floor where he lay.

'Who killed the man that impersonated Grimwig at the theatre?' Baynes asked.

'Him. Grimwig,' Quist answered. Baynes smiled broadly in triumph as if to say, *tell more*. 'He shot him in the alleyway leading to the flats a few minutes before the performance started. Set him up good and proper, so he didn't know what was happening before he did it. Paid him to dress up, gave him some cock and bull story about something or the other. Lured him to the archway and did him.'

'You were there?'

'I didn't know it was going to happen, I swear, Mr Baynes. Jacko knew. Him and Grimwig did it. It was Jacko who pretended to be his assailant afterwards.'

'And what about Archie Dibble?' Mary shouted.

'Yes, Mr Quist, tell us about Zielinski's murder,' Baynes said. 'Come, be quick, I'm sure Mr Furie has better things to do with his time.'

Quist looked over to the angry red face of Furie and quickly looked away, fearful of the glare given to him.

'Grimwig wanted the boy framed. Damn you to hell, Grimwig. We would have been away and free if it wasn't for your wish for revenge. He knifed Zielinski. He wanted false IOUs planted. I was to find them at the back of his ledger. Then, when we raided the Dibble's place, I was to go into the storeroom and pretend to find the money, glove and the knife. I had them concealed on me all the while. But it was him, that monster, he planned it all.'

'I need more, Sergeant Quist,' said Baynes, 'in case some clever lawyer with ambition contends you would say whatever it took to save your life. And I need it from your mouth, without any prompting. And so far, you've done well. Now the rest. Come on, you *were* a copper—a poor one for sure—but you know what is expected.'

Quist swallowed nervously as Furie shook him and leant him further past the forty-five-degree angle.

'All right, all right,' he screamed. 'For God's sake, don't let go.'

'My arm's getting tired,' Furie said.

'Jacko did the break-in. He burgled the pie shop and stole the knife, the ring and the glove. He said he knew exactly how to get in as his mate did it once before. Then Grimwig was to let the boy hang, and later he would see the girl dead as well. But only after she knew what he'd done and how she couldn't help her friend.'

Mary snarled at him and glared contemptuously at Grimwig. Her former employer cringed in pain while listening to Quist.

'But I swear, I didn't do the killings,' Quist said. 'My job at the theatre was to make sure that the doctor got away.'

'He was no more a doctor as you're a copper,' Mary shouted. 'He was a fake, wasn't he?'

Quist nodded.

Furie shook the policeman's leg back and forth. 'Answer the lady,' he growled.

'Dodds. Dodds. Bartholomew Dodds. He lives in Peckham. For God's sake, don't drop me.'

Baynes gave O'Connor a questioning look.

'Dodds is a con man. I know him well,' O'Connor confirmed.

By now, Quist was sweating and breathing heavily, frightened to look at either Grimwig or Jacko, more so, to look at Furie. His standing leg trembled with the strain, and he leant forward to grasp his burning thigh.

'Thank you, Mr Furie,' Baynes said. 'I have heard enough, for now.'

Furie smiled politely at the inspector. In a swift movement, he twisted Quist's leg and spun him around like a ragdoll, depositing him across the floor and against his friend, Jacko. He then brushed his hands together as if he was cleaning them of dirt. That done, he turned and came closer to Mary. He dwarfed the girl, standing a good two heads and a bit taller.

Immediately Tommy rushed to stand between him and her.

'Aren't you g-g-gonna arrest him?' Tommy said to the inspector, his voice trembling. He reached inside the cloth bag he carried and produced his grandfather's pistol, which he menaced at Furie. Tommy's face went white as he lifted the gun up. With both hands clutching the weapon, it shook, and he could barely steady it, it weighed so much.

'Y-you k-keep b-back, o-or e-else,' he stammered.

'Tiggs!' O'Connor and Byanes shouted.

A look of surprise came over the bare-knuckle fighter's face. His mouth dropped open in wonder. Before anyone could react, Furie reached out a swift hand and simply took the gun away, and Tommy fell back a step in utter astonishment.

'A Colt Dragoon!' he said. 'Benny. Look. A Colt Dragoon. I ain't seen one of those since I was a boy.' He scrutinised it carefully. 'Got any black powder, Benny?'

'And a shot maybe? Wait a second, I've a percussion cap somewhere,' Benny patted each of his pockets theatrically. 'Oooo, silly me, seems as if I'm not carrying any tonight.' He shook his head and rolled his eyes theatrically and grinned at Mary.

'A Colt Dragoon,' Furie repeated, thoughtfully. Nodding, he handed it back to Tommy. 'Son, you want to see that gets a clean and an oiling before you load and fire it,' he advised. Tommy received the gun, gingerly.

Mary edged closer to Furie, no longer fearing the man.

'I don't understand,' she said. 'I thought you were trying to kill me.'

The Imp came to stand beside her. She was slightly taller than him and that made her feel normal.

'Perhaps this will explain,' the Imp said, reaching inside his jacket pocket, he handed her a piece of paper.

Twisting it so it caught the moonlight, Mary read it several times.

'It's a telegram, from Mr Holmes.' She showed it to Mr Baynes.

WITH MILVERTON DEAD JAMES GRIMWIG WILL RETURN TO LONDON. HE WILL SEEK HIS REVENGE ON MARY FINCH. PROTECT HER. SHE IS TO BE FOUND AT THE ROSE GARDEN IN HOLLAND PARK. SHERLOCK HOLMES.

'We've been keeping him appraised,' Benny said. He clutched his lapels in a self-important way. 'He apologises and says his business has delayed him but he will return as soon as he can.'

'You know Mr Holmes?' Mary asked.

Benny slapped Furie's shoulder, though it was a reach. '*Fire-Fists* here's been giving him some pointers in the manly art of bare-fist boxing. Mr Holmes almost gave him a bloody nose.' Furie huffed his disbelief. 'But the big man gave him one first.'

'Couldn't miss that beak of his, even with my eyes closed, could I?' Furie said. He gripped his nose between thumb and forefinger and pretended to pull it out. 'Sticks out so much.' He boomed a laugh.

'We had a bit of a problem tracking you,' Benny continued. 'You weren't at the Rose Garden as Mr Holmes said, and it took a while to trace you to Lambeth. Then Furie sees you outside the sweetshop. And you were pretty fleet, so we've been a little behind at times.'

'But it was you that saved me on the bridge in the fog.'

Furie nodded.

'And a few times more you didn't know about,' Benny added. 'We been keeping an eye on you. We even put the word around for the bruisers to leave you alone. Most did. A few didn't. Furie saw to them.'

'Like the one who shoved me down the stairs in that store on Oxford Street.'

Benny drew a deep breath. There was a shy smile on his lips. 'Ah! Well, Miss, that was me that shoved you,' he admitted and shrugged a sorry. 'Razor Clarke was about to cut you bad so I had to do something. It was the best I could do at such short notice.'

'I had words with Clarke after,' Furie said.

'Let's say he's learned the error of his ways,' Benny added.

Mary swallowed drily, imagining the meaning behind the Imp's words. Her legs felt decidedly watery, and she could use a nice hot cup of sweet tea and a chair to sit on.

Instead, she thanked Furie and Benny and turned to the inspector.

'They're in it together,' she said of the men in his custody. 'I heard them say Jacko broke into Milverton's house a week after his death. He knew of another safe where Milverton kept his more profitable blackmail materials, hidden in the house.'

'I see,' Baynes said, nodding his understanding.

'And whatever he took is hidden somewhere in Grimwig's house,' Mary said.

'Grimwig said that?' Baynes asked and Mary nodded.

She paused, as if catching herself. Looking at the inspector who could barely conceal his smile, she huffed angrily, shook her head and ground her teeth. *And pigs will fly,* ' she hissed to herself.

Immediately, Mary went and crouched beside Grimwig. Ignoring his shooing hands, she rummaged through the man's pockets and pulled out an envelope that was stuffed full and roughly folded.

'Grimwig!' both Jacko and Quist shouted.

She handed it to Mr Baynes. The policeman looked at it, deep in consideration, turning it over and over in his hands.

'Inspector, you can't keep it,' Mary said. 'I mean, it's not right.'

Baynes shook his head. 'I have no intention of keeping it. Some things are best forgotten.'

He dropped the envelope to the ground and reached into his waistcoat pockets and found some matches.

'A little fire to keep you warm until the ambulance arrives, Mr Grimwig,' he said.

Striking the match on the floor and shielding the flame with his hand, he promptly set the envelope alight. Grimwig's expression dropped as he watched the envelope burn. In a few minutes, ashes were all that remained. Whatever was in there vanished in smoke.

Glaring at the inspector, Grimwig scowled. 'My brief will make short shrift of Quist's *confession*. It was still obtained under duress.'

Mary gritted her teeth and held back her anger. She knelt beside Grimwig, gripped one of his hands and turned it palm upwards.

'It's obvious Sergeant Quist never read any of Mr Holmes's monographs,' she said to the inspector. 'Otherwise, he'd have known about fingerprints and would have told Mr Grimwig to be careful. When you showed us the stuff Quist found under the floorboards in the Dibble's shop, I saw several fingerprints on the knife handle and on the money.'

'I am ahead of you, Miss Finch,' Baynes said.

'You checked the ones from the dead bloke in Charing Cross morgue, I noticed,' she said, remembering the blackened fingertips from the printer's ink he had used. Her observation drew a wry smile on Baynes's face. 'I reckon these will be the correct ones.'

'Oh, I would not bet against you,' the inspector said.

'Fingerprints? What the hell's that?' Grimwig said.

'You will discover soon enough, Mr Grimwig,' Baynes said. 'And I believe that Jacko will be more than happy to add to Mr Quist's statement when it is explained why he should.'

'After all,' Mary said, 'you did try and cheat them, why should he protect you?' She grimaced bitterly at him. 'Seems it's every man for himself now, Mr Grimwig.'

Even though the British courts had yet to accept fingerprints as evidence, Mary had no doubts concerning Inspector Baynes's powers of persuasion. And both Quist and Jacko's fears of the hangman, would seal Mr Grimwig's fate.

The utter contempt that Mary's former employer held for her was in the stare he returned.

28

CHRISTMAS AT THE ROSE GARDEN

IT SNOWED ON CHRISTMAS EVE. From her high vantage point, Mary watched fat flakes swirl and chase each other in the breeze and lay a thick blanket on roofs and streets, trees and walls. Nothing was spared from the coating of white. Overnight, it remade the world, turning it into a sparkling white dream.

The next day, Christmas Day, she set out early, happily walking through the drifts with a small bag slung across her shoulders. By chance, she was one of the first across Westminster Bridge early that morning. She turned, and her face lit up with impish glee to see the deep impressions of her footprints picked out starkly in the morning sunshine. Making her way to Baker Street, she knocked on the door of number 221B. Mrs Hudson informed her that Mr Holmes was still away. She left with her a small package to give to the detective upon his return, along with a second one for Dr Watson, who, also, was not there. Then she called in at the Dibbles.

Soon after, she left with Dot, Sossie and Archie, squeezed together warmly in a Hackney for Holland Park. Grandma and Grandpa Dibble would follow later.

The driver didn't complain about the crowding, instead wishing them the season's greetings as they climbed in. Before they could settle, though, Sossie dashed into the shop and came back a minute later. She held a large red apple for the horse and said a Merry Christmas to him for carrying them all. The driver had called him Sampson.

While neither wished to talk about recent events, Archie, nevertheless, wondered how Mr Grimwig would have carried out his blackmail from Argentina.

'I did what Mr Holmes does,' Mary said. 'I made some enquiries. Grimwig needed to get out of the country before Marshmere's case came before the courts. He probably though he'd have more time than he did. The last thing he wanted was his wife to be tangled up in a lengthy court case and maybe his scheme exposed. The single berth in first-class was for him. The ship was due to dock in Lisbon before crossing the Atlantic. He'd have a choice then. Either continue to Argentina, or wait in Lisbon until the fuss died down and come back to England via France. If they came back then they'd have traded their place on the ship with some other folks, so it looked as if they did go to the Argentine.'

Archie nodded his understanding. 'And when he came back, he'd have disguised himself, maybe grown a beard or something, and carried on as before.'

Why had Grimwig waited so long for his revenge on her? Much it seemed, came back to Milverton, and Grimwig's fears of what would happen to him should he harm someone, who he believed, worked for the master blackmailer. It was an odd twist of fate and showed how uncertain the future could be, that she should owe so much to Charles Augustus Milverton. Mr Holmes, though, foresaw it, and she was grateful that he acted accordingly.

Mary fell silent, not willing to speak any more about such times, and gazed out at snowy London, deep in thought. When they arrived at Mrs Grady's house, the girls charged ahead. The usual explosion of sound erupted when they met with their friends: Mrs Grady's ward, Ella Sutton, and the two maids of the same age she employed, Fortune and Kitty.

As soon as she walked through the front door, though, Mary sensed something was amiss. The house felt unusually quiet, despite the noise the children were making.

She peeked into the living room, looking for the old lady. The room was decorated with paper chains, and a tall Christmas tree stood next to one of the French windows. All sorts of ornaments hung off its branches, and ribbons were twirled and wrapped around it. On a nearby table, sat a mess of Christmas cards and notices of goodwill. The five girls were playing on the floor next to the fire, and Kitty's brother, Freddie, a fully-fledged member of the Baker Street Irregulars, was also there. Ella's mother and her grandma were there too. Grandma Sutton held a glass of sherry, and Mary was thankful that Ella's mother was only drinking tea.

Archie made his way to the tree and placed the armful of presents he brought under it.

Mary did the same and went to the dining room. The table was laid out for the Christmas meal Mrs Grady invited everyone to. Mary drifted into the morning room. It was empty. Again, she felt uneasy; a feeling she couldn't pin down troubled her. She went quickly to the kitchen, by far Mrs Grady's favourite place in the house. The old lady liked the warmth, the delicious smells of baking and the company of her friends, her cook, Eileen, and Mr Venables. Never one for ceremony, she would spend hours there chatting away.

Mrs Grady and Cook were not present, only Mr Venables and, surprisingly, Dr Watson. A woman she had never seen before was busy stirring a large pot bubbling away on the stove.

'Mr Venables, where's Mrs Grady,' Mary glanced at the woman by the stove, 'and Cook?'

Both men were holding glasses of sherry, and they placed them down.

'Mrs Grady is not here, Mary,' Mr Venables said. 'Nor is Eileen.'

'Not here?' Mary said confused.

Dr Watson pulled out a chair. Taking Mary's hand, he walked her over and sat her down. They sat beside her.

'I don't understand,' Mary said. She could see the seriousness in the men's faces.

'She has gone back to Ireland,' Mr Venables said.

'Back? But.' That feeling of unease returned, and Mrs Grady's strange conversation on the day she took Mary to her lodgings filled her mind. She sensed something was untoward then, something she didn't speak about, but something Mary put down to Mrs Grady's concerns about the lodging house and nothing more.

Mr Venables placed his hand on Mary's and drew nearer.

'Rosie asked me to tell you, Mary.' He squeezed her hand. 'She's said too many goodbyes in her life—friends and family and a husband. She's an old woman, and one more goodbye she couldn't stand. So, she and Cook have gone to Ireland. And I shall follow them before next year is out.'

'But, why?'

'Mrs Grady has put on a brave face,' Dr Watson said. 'But she never really recovered from the Denbie affair. It took a toll on her, mentally as well as physically.'

'She wanted to go home, Mary. She has been away far too long, she asked me to tell you that it was time to return.'

'But this is her home,' Mary said. She bit her lip. She could feel her tears welling up.

'It is *a* home,' Mr Venables said, 'but not *her* home. Her home is her father's old house in County Kerry. During the summer, she made enquiries and has recently completed the purchase. She and Eileen departed several days ago. With good train connections, they will be there by now.'

Mary sat quietly. She took several deep breaths. 'How ill is she?' she asked the doctor.

Dr Watson sighed. 'Mrs Grady has made her peace with the world,' he said.

Mary felt a hand on her shoulder and turned to see Archie standing beside her.

'Did you know?' she asked him.

'She told me the morning after I was released from jail,' he said. 'But asked me to not speak to you.'

'She was afraid her courage would fail if you knew,' Mr Venables said.

'What will happen now?' Mary asked.

'Mrs Grady has made arrangements,' Dr Watson said. 'She is a rich woman, and has always used her wealth to benefit others. The Rose Garden is to be converted into a home for destitute children. To accommodate as many people as possible, another house will be built on the grounds. It is to be no workhouse, Mary. Teachers will be hired, and those housed here will be educated. The chil-

dren will leave the Rose Garden with a skill. Employment will be found for them.'

'She would save the world if she could, Mary. You
know the woman as well as I,' Mr Venables said. 'This
will be a start. She said we shall save them one at a time
if necessary. I will remain a while and oversee the work.'

'Ella Sutton, Fortune Dubois and Kitty…' Dr Watson
smiled, he gazed upwards playfully, closing his eyes and
shaking his head, '*Short pants,* will be the custodians of
the charity when they reach their majority. Until then, I
and several others, including Mr Druze, will act as execu-
tors and guides. We will administrate and put the
endeavour on a sound footing, and afterwards act as advi-
sors. We will see that it prospers.'

'Rosie hoped that you might be part of her plans,' Mr
Venables said. 'But over the summer, she came to understand that your star leads elsewhere and you must follow
it wherever it goes.'

'And you will return to Ireland as well?' Mary asked
the butler.

'It is my time also, Mary. Eileen and I have known
Rosie for the best part of our lives; it is fitting we should
be together in the last part.' He withdrew an envelope
from his breast pocket. 'Rosie said you are to promise her
you will not be sad. The letter explains much.' He placed
it in Mary's hand. 'But do not read it today. Do it when
you have had time to think.'

Mary's eyes dropped. She clutched the letter carefully

and sniffed back her tears. She felt as if things would never be the same again. She'd known Mrs Grady for barely a year and already felt her loss as an ache in her heart. All her friends were leaving, or so she thought.

'You know what?' Archie said. He squeezed her shoulders. 'I'm gonna prove that old bat wrong and become prime minister one day. The Right Honourable Archibald Socrates Dibble, PM.' He posed pompously, and everyone laughed. Mary laughed along, simply because she felt she ought to and not show her sorrow.

Leaving the kitchen, she spent a few minutes wandering the upstairs corridor. She went to Mrs Grady's bedroom. The scent of the old lady's perfume still hung in the air. She sat on the stairs for a few moments, Oscar, her cat, beside her. Then she went outside and stood for a few minutes in the cold fresh air, in the garden where she and Mrs Grady talked that first time she came here.

'Now, tell me, will you accept the position of maid?' Mrs Grady asked. *'I can use a bright girl like you. Someone who can think on her feet and is brave and willing to take chances. A resourceful, clever girl, with some brains. It is an unfair world, and a harsh one for a child like you, Mary, orphaned and penniless. If the truth were known, it's just as harsh for an old lady like me, childless and alone. My best years are behind me. Yours are in front. We can help each other. You see, Mary, everyone's suffering is the same; it's just our devils that are different.'*

Mary knew that things change. Nothing ever stays the same. At that moment, she felt it keenly.

Suddenly, she screwed up her face and placed her hands across her ears. The noise, for what a noise it was, of Christmas carols assaulted the air, and rising a pitch above the others was Kitty's voice. Hers was a caterwaul, that of an enthusiastic banshee, that made Mary smile.

AUTHOR'S NOTES

The London Particular, also known as a pea souper, was a thick, often yellowish-greenish-blackish fog caused by air pollution and contained soot particles and the poisonous gas, sulphur dioxide. The very thick smog occurs in cities and is derived from the burning of coal for home heating and in industrial processes. Such a fog was injurious to health. Incidences of this type of fog date back to the 12th century. It would be after many years of the British population having to endure this deadly menace that the *Clean Air Act, 1956,* was passed, banning the use of coal for domestic purposes in urban areas. This chiefly came about when, a few years earlier, the worst recorded instance of such a fog happened: the *Great Smog of 1952.* It was estimated that some 4,000 people died in the city over a couple of days, and some 8,000 later on.

There have always been spies. It was during the Crimean War (in 1854) that the British War Office established the Topographical & Statistic Department, an embryonic military intelligence organisation. Its focus initially was on accurate mapmaking of sensitive, strategic locations and the collation of militarily relevant statistics. This was reorganised in 1873 as the Intelligence Branch of the War Office. Its brief was to *collect and classify all possible information relating to the strength, organization etc. of foreign armies... to keep themselves acquainted with the progress made by foreign countries in military art and science...*

By 1909, this became the Secret Service Bureau, an independent and interdepartmental agency fully in control of all government espionage activities. They have no policing powers, but liaise with the *Special Branch* of Scotland Yard. It contains nineteen military intelligence (MI) departments – MI1 through to MI19. The most well-known of these are MI5 and MI6.

Today we take fingerprinting for granted. It was in 1880 that Henry Faulds, a Scottish surgeon in a Tokyo hospital, published his paper on the use of fingerprints as an identification system. He proposed using printer's ink to record them on paper. He presented his concept to the Metropolitan Police force in London in 1886, but it was rejected. In 1892, Francis Galton published a detailed statistical model on fingerprint analysis and identification, *Finger Prints*. The chances of two people having identical prints, he calculated, were 64 billion to 1.

The first known case where fingerprint analysis was used to solve a case was in Argentina in 1892. When Francisca Rojas was found with neck injuries in a house where her two sons were found murdered, she claimed her neighbour was responsible. When, after severe interrogation, the neighbour did not confess, Juan Vucetich, the Argentine chief of police, visited the crime scene to find a bloody thumb mark on a door. The print matched Rojas, who confessed to the murder of her sons.

Some liberties have been taken in the writing of this book and in the use of fingerprinting as a crime solving technique. It was only in 1901 that British courts would accept fingerprints as evidence. In 1905, (the case of the Farrow Murders), Alfred and Albert Stratton were the first persons to be convicted of murder in the United Kingdom based on fingerprint evidence.

Sir Arthur Conan Doyle was quick to realise the importance of fingerprints as an identification system. Holmes used it in Doyle's 1890 book, *The Sign of Four*.

REVIEW REQUEST

PLEASE LEAVE A REVIEW

Please take a moment to rate and review **Mary Finch Endgame** as this helps others (kids and parents) discover the story.

Authors love to hear from their readers! Thank you!

To contact the author: saywackwrites@gmail.com

or for more information visit: https:saywackwrites.com

Facebook page: https://www.facebook.com/SSSaywack/